WHAT
LIES
THROUGH
THE
SMOKE

WHAT LIES THROUGH THE SMOKE

ENTER SMOKE CITY

C.C. FORD

First published in Great Britain in 2025

Editing, design, typesetting and publishing by UK Book Publishing.

www.ukbookpublishing.com

ISBN: 978-1-918077-38-4

CHAPTER ONE

A blimp passed underneath the archway which connected the Bowler Building to the Sunny Tower. The latter had been given its name because it was meant to be the only building tall enough in the city to sit above an almost ever-present layer of fog. Although, since its construction, other buildings had been built, each taller and more imposing than the last which made its name redundant. The city's wealthy architects had competed with one another to see who could design and build the tallest and most striking towers. However, in their pursuit for greed and bragging rights, they made it so only the most affluent could afford to inhabit them and drove the less privileged into shorter, less desirable structures. The most destitute of the city's inhabitants had little choice but to reside in the undercity. A maze of narrow streets, alleyways, markets and decrepit apartments.

The fog sat above these streets, blocking out most of the natural sunlight, while a vast network of highways, many lanes wide, connected the towers to one another. Inside the heart of many of the concrete monoliths were large car ports which allowed a constant influx of goods and people to come and go. Many of the tower dwellers had never seen grass nor any other kind of flora, unless it was on a picture screen or on an old painting. There wasn't much grass anymore, certainly not near the cities. The war and the near irreversible damage to the ecosystem had almost put an end to it.

Detective Inspector Harry Quinn stood on his balcony and sipped cheap black coffee from his metal mug; he wasn't sure if the water had been purified enough that morning as it left an odd aftertaste in his mouth. Although that could have been due to his hangover, which was slowly worsening the more the day went on. A half-drunk bottle of whisky lay on its side atop the kitchen counter, next to a chipped glass.

His braces hung from his hips; he had yet to finish getting dressed. After downing the rest of the unappetizing coffee, he took one last drag of his cigarette before flicking the butt over the railings where it would be lost in the fog many storeys below him.

Tossing the mug into the sink and pulling the braces over his shirt, he went to adjust them, but the picture phone rang. A call before he arrived at the precinct was never a good thing. It usually meant either a wealthy tower dweller had been murdered, or something expensive had been burgled and its rich owner wanted it back, pronto.

Harry walked across his apartment, knocking an empty glass of whisky off the coffee table as he fumbled to lift the hearing cone off the receiver before the call ended. He placed the cold brass cone against his ear and flicked the metal switch on at the base of the screen. A fuzzy black and white image appeared before him which eventually settled.

On the screen was a uniformed cop looking back at him, the black peak of his cap covering his forehead.

The officer took a step backwards and said, "Hello, is that Detective Inspector Quinn?"

"Yes. Good morning. I assume this isn't good news," Harry said, adjusting the picture on the screen so it looked less grainy.

"Sorry, sir, no. I have been asked to call you as we need a detective on the top floor of the Bilbury Building."

"And who lives on the top floor of the Bilbury Building?"

"Well, I don't think anybody now, sir – the owner was found dead by his secretary this morning."

"I see, and who is the recently departed?"

"It's the CEO of the Volster Corporation. This is some high-profile whack."

Harry almost smiled when he heard that term – the officer was clearly from the lower levels to use terminology like that. Like many cops, he probably had a young family at home and was doing his best to buy an apartment in one of the higher towers for them all so they could have a chance at a marginally better standard of living.

"So, Lucius Volster if I am not mistaken?"

"That's right, sir."

"How did he die?"

"Appears a slug through the back of the head, although there's something else you should know, sir."

"What is it?"

"There are a lot of strange markings on the walls of his office."

"How so?"

"You… you had better come down here, it would be easier in person."

"Alright, tell your sergeant I am on my way. Keep a log of everyone who comes and goes and keep the press out."

"Yes, sir."

Harry flicked the switch and the picture on the screen disappeared in a flash of white light. He placed the brass cone back on the hook and rummaged around his apartment to find a tie and his fedora. Rubbing his rough, unshaven face, he figured he didn't have time to do anything about it that morning. As he stepped out of his front door, he grabbed the small .38 calibre revolver that hung on the coat rack and stuffed it into the leather holster which sat across his waist. It didn't occur to him until he locked the door behind him that he wasn't even the on-call detective that morning. Somebody had asked for him directly. The uniform was right: this was a high-profile case, and Harry was never prepared for one. Nobody in the precinct liked working rich stiff jobs, it riled up the other tower dwellers who all thought they were next, or that there was a conspiracy to kill them all, which could only come from the depths of the undercity below them. Pressure was always placed on the department to catch the culprit quickly. Corners were regularly cut; procedures were breached, and lines were often crossed to catch the killer, who was usually just another wealthy socialite or businessman who had been screwed over in some trade deal and lost money. Harry considered himself an honest detective in a dishonest city – although he wasn't opposed to bribing a snitch for information and drinking on the job if it helped cure an increasingly common hangover.

Stepping into the rickety elevator, he pulled the stiff lever and stuffed his hands in his pockets while it slowly lowered. Keeping his head low, he tried to picture what he knew about the Volster Corporation. They were a construction firm, responsible for many of the highways which connected the city. But they also produced cars and trains, all of which ran on diesel. Why would anyone want to shoot the CEO in the back of the head, Harry wondered. The elevator clattered and made a worrying clunking noise as it arrived at the car port. Most high-rise buildings had a car port every ten floors or so. Car lifts were positioned on their edges where they could be raised or lowered onto the highways that ran directly through them.

Harry approached his car and rummaged through his trench coat pocket to find his keys. The two-seater cherry red roadster was aging like he was, although many of his colleagues still paid compliments to its curves, decent paint job and sleek design. It took a few seconds before the engine finally fired up and black smoke shot out of the exhaust. Harry stuck it in drive and pulled out of his bay and onto the car lift. The pressure plates were working today as the lift automatically lowered itself until it was on the slip road that connected to the highway. Traffic was light, which meant the air wasn't as foul as it usually was. Out onto the highway and heading into the depths of the city, the detective often imagined he was driving right into its polluted black heart.

CHAPTER TWO

The Bilbury Building stood tall amongst a trio of other striking towers that were connected by a string of highways. As with many of the towers, wealthy businessmen and women lived on the upper floors where they would stand and admire the city they had helped finance and build, and some that also helped corrupt and allow to fester. Harry drove into the centre of The Bilbury and pulled off the highway, onto the lift. He leant out the window and pulled the lever for the highest car port. Expensive looking limousines and sleek sportscars filled the bays. Indeed, rich folk resided in this tower, especially on the higher floors at least. Harry parked his roadster amongst a group of marked police cars. They hadn't been updated in years and made his own car look modern by comparison. Their black and white livery was dirty and tired. For years the city had been reluctant to invest in its police force, even if every mayor promised to do so during their election campaigns. The most recent pledged that he would end the scourge of the undercity and put more cops on the streets, yet had failed to do either of those things.

Harry stepped out of his car and locked it behind him. He climbed a wide set of concrete stairs towards one of the elevators. The sound of cars passing through echoed off the thick tower walls. A uniformed cop stood next to one of the elevator operators. His issued clothing was crisp and well maintained. The officer's leather knee-high boots were highly buffed along with the gold badge that glistened against his black uniform. A leather strap ran across his shoulder and connected to his belt. Against his hip was his service revolver and his long black truncheon sat on the other side. A set of chain handcuffs sat secured in their leather pouch. The crest on his eight-point cap also glistened in the light. This officer clearly took pride in his appearance like Harry used to when he wore the uniform. Years of working as a detective in the centre of Smoke City had knocked the enthusiasm out of him. He took a quick glance at his own scuffed brown shoes and made a mental note to slap a coat of polish on them when he got back home later that evening. That was if he remembered before he popped a fresh bottle.

Just like his shoes, the badge he presented to the uniform was also in need of some care and attention.

"Detective Quinn," Harry said, holding up his tarnished badge to the officer.

The uniform leant forward and inspected it. He nodded at the operator who stood aside and pulled the barrier open. His boots creaked; the officer must have been fresh from the academy.

"This way please, detective," the operator said, stepping into the lift.

"Thanks." Harry acknowledged the uniform as he stepped past him into the elevator.

The lift sounded smoother than the one in his own apartment building – the gears were clearly serviced more regularly. It was decorated with red paint and deep mahogany which ran across the edges of the ceiling.

The operator stood wearing a matching dark blue uniform with gold buttons, although his jacket wasn't buttoned correctly and looked as if it didn't fit him very well. A blue hat sat perched on his head. He was a couple of years younger than Harry and spoke slowly.

"Terrible thing what happened to Mr Volster," the operator said.

"How do you know about him?" Harry asked, lighting another cigarette and turning to look at the man stood beside him.

"Police have been coming and going all morning. Mr Volster usually leaves for the office early hours. Besides, your colleagues seem to forget I am standing behind them; they all talk and gossip."

"Do they now?"

"They do, sir; indeed they do."

"What do you know?"

"Not much, other than that he's dead. Shot in the head supposedly."

Harry took a long drag of his cigarette and asked, "Were you working last night?"

"No, that would be Reggie, he works the night shifts."

"I'll have to pay him a visit a little later on, see what he knows."

"You'll struggle."

"Why's that?"

"Reggie doesn't speak, hasn't done in years. People just tell him which floor, and he pulls the lever. I think he took ill when he was younger, and it affected his brain or something. He is a sweet boy though, always smiling."

"Right, thanks for the heads up. Where does Reggie live?"

"No idea, you'll have to ask the building clerks. They have access to his employment files. Am I a suspect in this, detective?"

"Yes. No. Maybe."

Harry took another drag of his cigarette before stubbing it out in a free-standing ash tray in the corner of the lift.

"What is your name?"

"Bernard, sir."

"You here yesterday, Bernard?"

"Yes, sir, finished at seven o'clock. That's when Reggie took over."

"And was Mr Volster alive then?"

"I guess so, took him up to his floor that evening."

"What time exactly?"

"Around six o'clock like usual. Mr Volster usually arrives home around this time unless there is heavy traffic. But he often works late into the night. He is a busy man, you see. Always taking his work home with him."

"Does he live alone?"

"No. He has lived with his adopted daughter since his wife died some time ago."

"I was informed that his secretary found him. Does she live with him also?"

"Yes, well his secretary is his adopted daughter, you see. He pulled her from the undercity when she was just a child. Raised her as his own."

"Does he have any biological children?"

"Yes, two. Horus and Jasper. Jasper hasn't been seen for some time though."

"What happened to him?"

"Got addicted to that drug down in the undercity."

"He's a fumer?"

"If that's what they call it. Yeah, went down one day and never came back. He is alive though."

"How do you know?"

"Collects the money that Mr Volster wires to him every month. Guess that'll stop now though. He may even make an appearance once he figures out the cash has stopped."

The lift came to a slow crawl before stopping. The operator opened the gate for Harry and gestured for him to step through. He would have tipped him if had some loose cash. He could always claim it back from the department if they had some lying around, although it meant filling out frustratingly complicated forms

"Thanks. I am not sure how long I will be. I will probably see myself out," Harry said, stopping to speak to the operator.

"No problem, detective."

"If you hear anything or find out anything, please do call me."

Retrieving a crumpled and cheap looking business card which were standard issue for all detectives, he handed it to the operator. They smiled at one another before the detective turned and walked towards the huge set of wooden doors in front of him. Two other uniforms stood either side, both as well dressed as the one downstairs.

Harry raised his badge again and nodded at them both. They turned and opened the doors, which creaked loudly as Harry stepped forward into the grand penthouse apartment. On either side of the walls were tall bookcases filled with numerous leatherbound books, each accompanied by a tall ladder. A grand piano stood against the large glass windows that overlooked the city. Expensive leather sofas, side tables and ornaments filled the rest of the entrance. The duty sergeant was stood talking to another officer. He was broader than the other cops, looking stocky and weathered. A scar ran across his left cheek, and his nose was red from years of drinking hard liquor. Like many seasoned cops, it was probably the only thing that got him through a shift. Harry recognised him and had seen him around the precinct before but never got his name. The sergeant noticed the detective admiring the impressive interior and slowly walked towards him. His footsteps were heavy, which only made his demeanour more imposing. No doubt the young officers both feared and respected him.

"Detective. I'm Sergeant Murillo, the supervisor for this district," he said.

"Good morning, sergeant. Detective Quinn. How you doing?" Harry said, reaching for another cigarette.

"Better than the poor son of a bitch who owned this place. Come on, I'll take you to him."

Harry flicked the lid on his lighter and pressed the flame against the cigarette which hung from his lips. He stuffed it back into his pocket and followed the sergeant into another room. The walls on either side were covered with portraits of nobilities of old. Unable to recognise most of them, but the ones he did were the founders of Smoke City. Engineers and architects who had built the city from the ground up. They started with the factories and houses, which soon became crowded and polluted. They realised that the wealthy needed somewhere better to live and so began the construction of the towers and the upper city. The undercity became an afterthought to them. Even as the inhabitants continued to slave away in the factories and refineries which powered the city and made their lavish lifestyle possible.

At the far end of the room, in the centre, was a wide wooden desk. Slumped over it was the corpse of Lucius Volster. Paperwork was scattered all over the desk and the floor beneath his lifeless body. Dicky, the crime scene photographer, was capturing images of the scene. He got his nickname as he always sported a crooked dickie bow which hadn't been considered fashionable for years. Some of the officers joked that he couldn't make the grade shooting for the press and only knew how to frame a corpse. He was short and skittish and rarely spoke. When he did, it was in quick fire sentences which made some of the more jovial officers laugh and tease him.

The detective and the sergeant walked towards the desk until they were close enough to get a good look at the departed. Blood was splattered all over the varnished wooden top along with the sheets of paper scattered on it. An exit wound was present in the front of his skull. He had been shot at close range through the back of the head. A fountain pen was still clutched in his right hand. Lucius Volster was one of Smoke City's oldest residents. At eighty-seven, he was practically ancient in a city where many didn't reach seventy. The fog, pollution and sickness often put a halt on people making old bones, despite the wealthy having access to the best medicine money could buy.

It wasn't the wound and blood that caught Harry's eye, but a symbol which had been scribbled on every piece of paper on the desk. It looked like a black tube with a spiral above it. Harry picked up one of the sheets and examined the symbol.

"You ever seen anything like that before?" Sergeant Murillo asked.

"No. You?" Harry said, not taking his eyes off the symbol.

"No, and neither have any of my guys. Hey, Dicky. Dicky!"

Dicky stopped shooting and looked at the sergeant with his beady eyes.

"You ever seen this symbol before?"

"What symbol?" Dicky snapped.

"The symbol on every piece of paper you have been looking at through a lens for the last half hour."

"Oh. That symbol. Nah."

Dicky stuck his eye against his camera and went back to shooting the scene and stopped paying attention to the sergeant.

"I'll tell you what it is," a voice said, coming from the other side of the room.

Harry turned to see who it belonged to and was surprised to see a beautiful young woman walking towards him. Her hair was a deep red which matched her shade of lipstick. She sported a black and white polka dot dress and walked in heels the way a woman should do. The sound of them hitting the wooden floor was only interrupted by the sound of the flash from Dicky's camera as the other men stood and admired her in a shared silence.

"Detective, this is Victoria, Lucius' daughter," the sergeant said.

"Ma'am," Harry said, removing his hat.

Victoria looked the detective up and down and said, "So you're the man who is going to catch my father's killer, huh?"

"I intend to try, ma'am."

"I don't want you to try. I want you to find him."

Harry paused and took a drag of his cigarette. He admired the woman's confidence and attitude. It reminded him of his wife.

"What can you tell me about the markings?"

"They are from a group down in the undercity. A cult more like."

"Does this cult have a name?"

"They go by The Children of the Smoke. Have you heard of them?"

"No. Should I have?"

"They are becoming a problem for us. They have sent many threatening letters to our company, and we believe they are responsible for some recent sabotages to our factories."

"Threats and smashed windows are a far cry from murder."

"I am aware, detective, but this is their symbol. It is a smokestack. They claim to all be children of the undercity who grew up never seeing sunlight."

"Have you ever seen one in person?"

"Nobody in the towers have."

"Ma'am," the sergeant interrupted, "we have cops in the undercity, good ones. And I have never heard one of them mention one of the smoke kids or whatever they are called."

Victoria gave the sergeant an icy stare and said, "I assure you, sergeant, they are real. I suspect they are probably only in their infancy; I fear this won't be the last murder."

Harry looked at the empty ashtray on the blood-stained desk and stubbed his cigarette out on it. He turned his gaze back towards Victoria and said, "For someone who is stood in the same room as her dead father, you are taking it pretty well, Ms Volster."

"I am not one to cry, nor am I one to become overly emotional. You see, detective, my father taught me to be strong and hardy, no matter the situation you are presented with. This is why he was so successful and achieved so much."

She was as believable as she was stoic, although he could hear a faint hint of sadness in her voice. She was probably giving her all not to shed a tear or show a hint of weakness to the men stood in her adopted father's study.

"You found him, didn't you?"

"Yes, he didn't arrive for work this morning, He wasn't answering the phone, and this was totally out of character for him. Punctuality is very important to my father."

"Is the lift the only way onto this floor?"

"Besides the stairs. Yes. Although that's not to say someone couldn't do something crazy like jump from a blimp or scale the walls."

"Reggie, the lift operator, was on last night, wasn't he?"

"Yes. He works the night shifts unless it is his day off."

"Sounds like we need to pay him a visit."

"You'll struggle."

"I know, he is a mute."

"Who told you that?"

"The elevator operator on this morning, Bernard I think he said his name was."

Victoria paused for a moment, her expression turned to one of concern and confusion before she said, "He was sent home first thing when I found the body. He was overcome with grief. Who have you been talking to?"

Harry and Murillo shared a look and then bolted towards the exit to the study.

"You! With me!" Murillo shouted at the other uniform stood by the entrance to the apartment. He followed swiftly even if he didn't know why. The officers made their way back to the elevator. Harry pulled the handle and drew his revolver. The others also drew their service weapons and pointed them at the lift's doors. It felt like an eternity before Harry heard the lift approaching. The small gun he gripped tightly was becoming heavier, and his hand began to shake. As the doors opened, Harry cocked the hammer but trembled when he saw the young officer slumped dead against the walls of the elevator. The blood was difficult to see against the red paint, despite it being splattered all over it. His throat had been slashed from ear to ear. Scribbled on the walls was the same symbol Harry had seen in Lucius' study.

Harry de-cocked his revolver and stuffed it back into his holster. He turned and looked at the uniforms behind him who were both as white as the fog which sat beneath them. They lowered their revolvers and looked at Harry who was lost for words.

Standing between both the startled uniforms, Victoria said, "Now do you believe me, detective?"

CHAPTER THREE

After Harry made a call for a second body collector to attend, he slowly made his way back to his car. Another elevator had to be used as he couldn't bear riding in the same one as that poor cop had. Once he was back out of the building and in the car port, he lit a cigarette and admired the infrastructure of the tower. Art Deco had become the norm for many of the towers. It seemed to be the only stylistic choice for Smoke City, even down in the undercity. Nearly every building was made from reinforced concrete, and an emphasis was placed on their verticality, flurry of windows and stylized sleekness of curves. The interiors of many apartments and office buildings shared similarities including the furniture choice. The same style of couches, side tables and lamp shades were present wherever he went. Many of them sporting bold colours which contrasted with the almost constant grey atmosphere that washed over the city. Some of the buildings tried to separate themselves from the usual designs but stuck out, and were quickly overshadowed by the construction of bigger, more aesthetically pleasing buildings. His apartment building wasn't considered to be high or exuberant enough to be a tower, but it was tall enough to sit above the fog, even if he felt like he could almost touch it from his balcony sometimes.

Slowly walking back to his roadster, he made a mental note to buy another pack before going home that night. His tin was almost empty. Before unlocking his car, he walked towards the edge of the platform and looked down at the highway below him. The traffic had picked up now. Large trucks had started making their runs into the city, carrying goods to and from the towers and factories which were in abundance in the outskirts. Many sported long curved bonnets and narrow windscreens along with tall exhausts that produced a constant stream of black smoke. Most were indistinguishable from one another. Their company logos and trailers they towed were obscured and covered in black dust. Occasionally some yellow lettering could be made out beneath the dirt.

Harry often wondered what life was like outside the city, whether the air felt smoother and the water tasted better. Like all residents, he supplemented his diet with nutrient pills and God knows what else his doctor had ordered him to take. He could count on one hand how many times he had left the city; each time it was to follow a lead or track down a suspect. Yet every time he drove beyond the city boundary, he couldn't wait to come back. The surrounding wasteland left little to admire, although he had heard stories of lush fields and forests further out west from travellers who frequented the city's bars. Like many of the residents, he had never seen a forest and doubted he ever would. Once Harry had finished smoking his cigarette, he flicked it off the edge of the platform and walked back to his car. Knowing he'd have to make a trip to the precinct, he started the engine, and his suspicions were reaffirmed when the car's dashboard started to beep and a red light flickered. He lifted the phone from the mount and stuck it to his ear.

"Detective Quinn," he said, resting his other arm against the door.

"Detective, it's Sergeant Boyle from the downtown, the commissioner is here and wants you down here right away."

"I thought I would be needed, tell him I am on my way."

"You got it."

Harry placed the phone back onto the mount and started his engine. He was about to pull away when he saw Victoria walking towards him. Part of him wanted to just leave and claim ignorance, but another part of him wanted to speak to her again, to admire her beauty and hear her soft yet strong voice. He decided to stay and lowered the window.

Reaching into her purse, Victoria said, "Detective, I just wanted to give you this before I go." She handed him a folded sheet of paper.

"What is it?" Harry said, taking hold of the sheet in between his fore and middle finger.

"My number, I want you to keep me updated on the case please. Any names or places I want to know. Reggie's address is also on there."

"I will tell you what you need to know, Ma'am, I can't have you interfering with this investigation. I assure you I will do what I can and keep you updated accordingly."

"Have you ever had a loved one be taken from you, detective?"

Harry paused and broke eye contact with Victoria, he composed himself and said, "Yes, once."

"And how did it feel when you couldn't get the answers you wanted?"

"Infuriating."

"Exactly, and I am not saying this to be difficult. I have access to places and people that may be able to help us catch my father's killers. Volster has resources at its disposal. I can get you into places you would usually struggle to without going through the correct procedures which I know take time."

"What sort of people?"

"People that are willing to do things you can't, or wont."

"What sort of things?"

"I don't need to spell it out for you, detective, just that I care more about bringing justice to my father than following the law, although you strike me as the sort of man who would bend the rules to do the right thing."

"What gave you that idea?"

"The way you carry yourself, you have yet to say anything you needn't, it's like everything you have done so far is with purpose."

"I am just doing my job, ma'am."

"It's Harry, isn't it?"

"Yes."

"Good, stop calling me ma'am, anyway, I need to go to the office. I will need to notify the company and the press. I will also need to call his son, Horus, and tell him the terrible news. The company will be turned upside down because of this. There will be a power struggle. Selfish men will use my father's death as an opportunity to further their own gain, to seize more power within the company."

"It sounds like you have your work cut out for you, Victoria."

"Probably still less than you do, Harry. Promise me you will call me if you find anything."

"I…I promise."

Victoria leant forward and said, "Good. I look forward to seeing you again, Harry."

The smell of her sweet perfume was in the air again; he noticed her eyes were an emerald green which he almost lost himself in. She stood up and walked away from his car and didn't turn to look back at him. Once he could no longer see her, he pulled out of the bay and headed towards the lift.

The downtown precinct stood in a group of taller buildings. It was as if the private companies that built them did it on purpose to remind the police that they were the ones with true power, and that they ran the city. The building's roof was flat so that police blimps could land on it. Many were seen at night patrolling the skies, the spotlights searching the networks of highways and communal areas above the fog. Crime was still present in the upper city; not all who lived there were excessively wealthy and some became desperate enough to turn to crime to pay the bills. Robberies, vandalism and lewd behaviour was still present. Criminals from the undercity would often sneak their way up past elevator checkpoints to hold up banks and steal motor vehicles which would quickly be stripped for parts or sold on.

It was no secret that extra time and resources were spent on victims who had healthier bank accounts; pressure from the mayor and city officials made sure of that. Harry was expecting a task force to be waiting for him when he arrived at the precinct, although the department had been bled dry over the last few years, and they were still waiting on the promise that the newly elected mayor made for more cops and better funding.

The building became visible in the distance as he cruised the busy highway. Giant letters fixed to the front of the building spelt S.C.P.D. It had large elevators than ran directly into the undercity, where prisoner trucks would roll out daily and return once full. Each shift, squads of cops would head out on foot into the undercity to maintain what little law and order was left. Sometimes not all would return. Street gangs roamed the narrow roads and alleys, often violent and greater in their numbers than the officers. Shootings were a daily occurrence and were seldom reported by the press unless an innocent bystander was caught in the crossfire, or a cop was killed. Lucius Volster's untimely demise would make tomorrow's headlines and tonight's news. The poor cop in the elevator would be lucky to get his own article and would likely just get a fleeting mention in the Volster story.

As the roadster cruised into the precinct, three squad cars shot out, lights and sirens on full blast, one sounded as if it was waning and malfunctioning. It used to be that only the newest and most pristine cars were allowed to patrol the towers, but due to budget cuts the department had little choice but to send whatever they had available out of the gates. Harry found a spot on a platform and reversed his car between an armoured truck and a squad car. The department no longer had designated cars for detectives, and now the best they could do was spare some petty cash for fuel and toll allowances. Most detectives fiddled the books to claim more than they were entitled to – it was an open secret that nobody cared about.

He shared the elevator with two uniforms but didn't recognise either of them. They both looked young and fresh; neither spoke, although Harry could hear the leather of the newly issued boots creaking. He reminisced about his time wearing the get-up. Patrolling the undercity where he learnt his craft, where he had made his first arrest and met his wife. He thought about Caroline until the lift arrived at the detective's floor. Nodding at the two uniforms and stepping out of the elevator, he found himself stood in the detective's area which was brimming with activity. A haze of cigarette smoke sat above the desks that cluttered the bustling room. Phones were constantly ringing, and the sound of reports being furiously typed made it hard to hear one's thoughts. Each detective had their own desk. Their speciality was engraved on a brass sign which sat on the front of it. Most worked homicide, although there were desks for fraud, robbery and rapes. The women were often assigned to work rape cases. Homicide was seen as a man's job, unless the case involved a sexual element then the women would be brought on in a consultant role, regardless of their ability. In the corners of the room were small offices where the department supervisors sat, rarely leaving unless they had to attend a meeting or visit the commissioner.

Harry's supervisor, Detective Chief Inspector David Carter, was a firm and fierce man. He had gained a reputation in his youth for having little patience for both suspects and witnesses, yet he cleared cases and soon climbed the ranks. He had made detective in less than five years and garnered fame when he caught a killer who had stalked the streets of the undercity and harvested the organs of his victims. Each time they killed, they left piece of paper with a different marking on it. Carter had put the markings together and recognised the symbol as belonging to a medical clinic in the entertainment district. The suspect turned out to be a doctor addicted to fuming who wanted to create the perfect being. Carter had shot and killed him when the mad doctor came at him with a scalpel. He wrote in his report that the doctor had verbally expressed interest in harvesting his ears and nose.

Harry started across the room, towards Carter's office, ducking and moving between desks to avoid hurrying detectives and clerks carrying heavy stacks of reports. He glanced at those he was friendly with, and they raised their hands in reply to acknowledge his presence. Most were busy holding a phone against their ear or typing, some holding a cigarette between their fingers. Peeking through the glass into Carter's office, he saw both Commissioner Harris and his aide stood by his supervisor. The aide, Lionel Beek, was a short, difficult man who wanted nothing more than to rise through the ranks and bury anyone in his way if they slowed his ascension. He was more of an administrator than a cop and what little time he'd spent in uniform was wasted on pointless investigations and projects. He avoided physical conflict wherever he went, and his arrest record was certainly lacking for a man of his position. Saying all the right things and laughing at all the right jokes was what many suspected had landed him his current position. Harry and Lionel shared little respect for one another, which they made openly clear whenever they had the displeasure of interacting with each other.

Harry took a deep breath and banged on the glass door. Carter waved to him to step inside.

"Come in, Harry, take a seat," Carter said.

Stepping into the office, removing his hat, Harry said, "Good morning, sir, good morning, commissioner." He purposely ignored Beek.

"Good morning," the commissioner said.

"Now, Harry," Carter said, "I am sure you are wondering why you were called this morning to pick up the Volster case given that you weren't the on-call detective."

Harry pulled a wooden chair out away from the desk, sat down and placed his hat on the wooden tabletop and said, "It did cross my mind, sir, where is O'Neil?"

"Dead."

"What?"

"Ate his own gun last night."

"God, he had a wife and kid."

"They both left him last month, ran off with a chauffeur who drove for a wealthy socialite uptown."

"Damn, he didn't deserve that, he was a good cop."

"He was, but truth be told he had slipped in recent years, and you were always going to be my first choice for this case."

"Why me, sir? If you don't mind me asking."

"Because every time you get a case you do nothing else except work it. And I can't remember the last time you asked me to file one without a conviction. How many killers have you caught since working in the department?"

"More than a dozen, sir."

"That's right and Commissioner Harris over here has taken interest in your record."

The smoke being blown up his ass by his boss was thick but expected. Carter was unlikely to say he was both job drunk and a regular drunk, who had no family, no woman and nothing else in his life to pull his focus away from his work. It was flattering, but Harry knew the truth as to why he was here.

"Detective Quinn," the commissioner said, "I don't need to tell you the importance of solving this case quickly. Lucius Volster was personal friends with the mayor. His family helped build this city. In fact, it was his company that laid the very foundations of the building we sit in now. His murder has gotten several other influential people worried. Talks of a cult murder from the undercity doesn't sit well with folk up here."

Harry looked at the commissioner sitting beside him. His impeccably pressed blue suit and bulled shoes put Harry's ragged appearance to shame. If he'd known he was meeting the commissioner today he would have at least chosen a better tie. The commissioner was a tall, lean man, his dark skin contrasting with his greying sideburns. Having only met him on a handful of occasions, he had never been addressed directly by him. He was more of a politician now than a police officer. It was more common to hear him on the radio giving interviews with journalists than talking to cops.

"Sir, I appreciate the department's faith in me, but wouldn't it make more sense setting up a task force for this case?"

The commissioner nodded and said, "I would love to offer you that, detective; however, we are operating on a shoestring budget. If you find any leads or come across anything then feel free to put a request in and we will see what we can spare. I am sure you are fully aware that we don't have the resources at the moment to set up a squad. I would like to offer you more support."

"I understand, sir." Harry turned his attention back to his chief inspector and said, "What do we know about this cult?"

Carter opened a drawer and retrieved a thick paper file. He chucked it onto the tabletop which almost knocked Harry's hat off and said, "This is everything we have on them so far. We think they have a base somewhere in the undercity's entertainment district or at least they have been seen to operate down there. They are new on the scene. Inside is every report that has been made by the attending officers. We even managed to get a photo of one of them, although the quality isn't the best. I want you to study this file, and tomorrow I want you to head down there and see what you can find. You report directly to me on this one. Don't make any moves unless you have my say-so."

Harry hated being kept on a leash – he was good at getting results because he was often given carte blanche when it came to an investigation. He seldom needed to request support or run an investigation by the brass. As long as a suspect was brought in, they usually didn't care how or why.

"Sir, with respect, I usually don't report unless I have a suspect."

"I know, Harry, but this case has some powerful people spooked. I don't want panic and rumours spreading around the towers."

"And what about the undercity?"

Carter leant back into his chair and stared deeply at Harry. He rubbed his face and said, "Harry, you don't need me to tell you that the undercity is often a law unto its own. We do what we can to protect the people down there. If anything, we give them too much and get little in return. Just do what you can down there with them and look after yourself. Feel free to utilise some petty cash if you need it. Money talks in those parts as I am sure you know."

Harry leant forward and picked up the thick file.

"Now, Harry," Carter said. "If you can excuse us."

Smiling at the men in the room, he retrieved his hat and took his leave. Beek gave him an acid stare as he walked past. He shut the door gently behind him. The last thing he saw of Carter was him tilting the wooden blinds so nobody could see into his office. This rarely meant good news. Neither did an appearance from the commissioner.

Once he had carried the file back to his desk, he removed the binder and began to study the contents, but not before lighting a cigarette. A dozen reports were made, varying from petty graffiti to industrial sabotage. Each time the same symbol was left behind: the smokestack. The first report was barely a month old but already the estimate was over one million dollars in damage. Mainly to the factories and fuel refineries on the outskirts of town. Their attacks had ranged from deliberate fires, damaged machinery and on one occasion, a homemade explosive which nearly brought a refinery to its knees. The sole image of one of the cult followers was grainy. A photo had been taken of a food stall in the undercity, seen in the corner, stood by an alleyway was a tall figure with a shaved head, wearing a long dark robe. The image was in black and white, but an inscription scribbled on the back of the photo said the robe was a dark red. The photo was dated Tuesday 9th September, one day short of a week ago. Harry opened a drawer and flicked through a stack of notebooks he had lying around. He flipped through the sheets until he came across a list of known snitches and informants who loitered in the entertainment district. It had been some time since Harry had been down there and he couldn't be sure if they were still alive, let alone still informing. One name in particular stuck out to him: Joel. He knew almost every street hustler, and gang member out there. If something or someone new was in the entertainment district, Joel would know about it.

Harry leant back in his chair and took a long drag of his cigarette. Across the room were other stressed and overworked detectives also sucking on the life shortening sticks of nicotine. One had held his still for so long whilst his head was pressed against the phone that it was nothing more than a thin streak of grey powder, begging to be flicked into an ashtray. After Harry was done browsing the file, he reached into his coat pocket and pulled out the piece of paper that Victoria had handed him; on one side was her phone number, the other was the address for the night operator, Reggie. Harry figured he had better check in on him and try and find out what he knew. Hopefully there would be someone there to translate for him – if not, perhaps Harry could get Reggie to write down who and what he saw, if he could write that was.

Reggie didn't live in the undercity. Like Harry, his apartment building stood above the fog; it wasn't a lavish tower by any means, but it meant Harry didn't have to go take a long ride down to visit him. He scribbled the apartment number into his notebook and flipped it shut.

CHAPTER FOUR

R eggie's apartment building was about a thirty-minute drive from the precinct. Harry had planned to use the time to think about the case, instead his mind drifted to Victoria – he thought he had caught a brief whiff of her perfume which must have been left on the door, the smell was quickly replaced by exhaust fumes as he cruised the highway. Briefly distracted, he admired a blimp flying overhead along with the metro rail line which ran below him. Smoke City, despite its problems, was a magnificent spectacle of architecture and ingenuity. It had inspired several other cities to follow and try and imitate its design, each with varying degrees of success.

Sewage and air quality were some of the biggest problems that plagued the city. The life expectancy for the city's inhabitants was dwindling, and despite the recent advancements in medicine, little could be done for many people who developed respiratory diseases just from simply breathing the air.

Arriving just before noon, Harry made his way onto Reggie's floor and found himself standing in a long corridor, a couple of lights flickered as he walked towards the apartment in question. The carpet was worn and needed replacing; the grey paint was peeling from the walls. Still, Harry had been in worse buildings in his time and this one almost reminded him of his own. As he approached the door, he noticed it was ajar. He pushed it open slightly and saw a mirror had been knocked off the wall. Shards of glass littered the area around it. Harry drew his revolver and pushed the door open entirely. Neither the lock nor the frame had been damaged. Whoever had entered had done so without resistance.

"Police! Anyone in here?" he shouted, although he wasn't expecting a reply from Reggie. He had remembered he was a mute, but when an officer announced their presence there was often a sound of scurrying or windows opening. Hearing nothing, he stepped into the small apartment, gun in hand. As he stepped around the corner into the living room, he saw the smokestack symbol drawn all over the walls. The place had been flipped, what little furniture there was had been broken and thrown around the room. Pictures lay smashed on the rug. Reggie's sofa bed was extended and took up most of the floor space.

"Reggie! Are you here?"

Nothing. He stepped into the kitchen which had also been trashed. Plates and other crockery had been smashed into pieces and littered the tiled floor. A knife sat on the counter with blood on it but there was no body in the room to link it to. The bathroom was untouched, the fight hadn't made it in there. After placing his gun back in its holster, he stood in the middle of the ruined apartment and stared at the biggest of the symbols which had been crudely drawn on the wall. Poor Reggie – if he was truly mute like people said then he wouldn't have been able to cry out for help. Harry banged on the neighbours' doors to see if they had heard or seen anything, but he got no reply. Calling cards were stuffed under them in the hopes that one would be courteous enough to give him a call. Once back at his car, he radioed through to file a missing person report and to get some uniforms down there to secure the scene. After he'd made the call, he went back to the apartment and rummaged through the mess to see if he could find anything that would help him find Reggie. He sieved through loose paperwork but found nothing other than bills and letters from whom he assumed were relatives. Checking his wardrobe, the detective noticed his work uniform was missing; it must have been how the killer had acquired their disguise.

This case was getting worse by the minute; he considered calling Victoria but thought against it. He didn't want her involved despite her wishes. He also didn't need the distraction nor another person to appease. The chief inspector and commissioner were more than enough. Once he felt he had spent long enough trying to find a clue as to Reggie's whereabouts, he went to find a picture phone in the hallway. After throwing some coins into the slot, he dialled Carter's number. It rang for a couple of moments before Carter's face filled the screen.

"Harry? You found something already?" Carter said.

The line was poor which made the audio out of sync with his boss's lip movements. The sound quality was also terrible. Harry pressed the cone hard against his ear and stuffed a finger into his other one.

"Sir, I paid a visit to Reggie's place. He isn't here; the place is a mess. I think… I think he has been taken, sir. There are symbols all over the walls. His uniform is missing. A knife in the kitchen has some blood on it, there was a real struggle it seems."

"All right, I take it you have searched the place. Neighbours see anything?"

"Nobody has answered their doors. I have left a calling card for a couple of them."

"Good, tell you what, Harry. I will get some uniforms down there to do a wider check, see if anyone in that building knows something about what's going on. But Harry…"

"Sir?"

"I hate to say this, but the priority is catching Volster's killer and finding this cult."

"I get that, sir, but if I can get something on Reggie, hopefully it will lead me to the cult."

"Or maybe it'll lead you to his body. So far we have only seen that symbol every time someone turns up dead, or something is destroyed. You said you found a bloody knife, Harry. It doesn't sound good."

"No, sir, it doesn't. I uh…I'll need to look deeper into the file and see what we have at all on this cult. Tomorrow I'll go below the fog. There has got to be something down there for me to find."

"Take the rest of the day off, Harry. Prepare yourself for tomorrow. No doubt you'll be on your feet for hours."

"I'll keep you posted."

The call ended and the screen went dark. Typical brass, not caring about the little person – it was almost as if nothing ever seemed to change. Carter didn't have to be so damn open about the case's priorities. Harry hung the cone back on the hook and waited for a uniform to show up. The one that did was older and fatter than the others he had met today, probably not far off his pension and seemed far less interested than Harry had expected. He explained the situation to the grumpy cop who scribbled a couple of lines into his notebook. That was enough for one day; he needed a drink despite it being the early afternoon. Once back on the highway, he tuned the radio until it picked up a jazz channel. The sounds of saxophones and drums washed over him before remembering he needed some cigarettes for the long day ahead of him. Finding a street vendor, he bought two packs along with some dried pasta and a bottle of bourbon. A rarity to do a full grocery shop these days. It was just him now and he often pacified his hunger with booze and nicotine.

Once home, he kicked his scuffed shoes off and carried the bottle under his arm towards the kitchen. He threw the bag of pasta and the file onto the cluttered kitchen counter. He poured himself a drink and downed it before pouring himself another. Harry carried the glass back into his living room and placed it on the table. Before sitting down, he went over to his safe which was hidden inside a sideboard and twisted the dial until it opened. He retrieved a bundle of cash notes along with a .45 semi-automatic pistol. He took out two clips and slammed the safe's door shut. It would be stupid to go knocking about the undercity without any extra firepower, especially the places he would be visiting and the people he would be dealing with. Snitches and informants tended to hide away in the roughest joints and liked to surround themselves with undesirable people, especially if they knew Harry was a cop.

Before returning to his couch, he placed a record on the turntable and found a groove with its stylus. More jazz, this time slower and more sombre than what he'd listened to on the drive home. He opened a drawer in a cabinet and retrieved a leather pouch. Once sat back on his couch, Harry unravelled it and emptied its contents onto the table. Stripping the, .45, he cleaned and oiled it. It had been a long time since the pistol had been fired, and he couldn't remember the last poor soul who had found themselves on the receiving end of his gun. He used to be able to remember them all. Once he reassembled the pistol, he loaded it, racked the slide and did a press check to ensure the round was chambered correctly and reapplied the safety. Leaning back on his sofa, he took a sip from the glass and rubbed his thick brown hair. His thoughts drifted to Lucius Volster and the poor young officer, then to Reggie and his whereabouts and whether he was even still breathing. Lastly, he thought about Victoria. About the way she carried herself with confidence and calmness, despite standing in the same room as her dead father. She gave Harry the impression she was capable yet also delicate. Her thick red hair and voluptuous figure then came to mind.

As much as he was hesitant to, he knew he needed to study the file some more. He retrieved it from the counter and sat and stared at the black and white photos of the symbols, along with the grainy image of the suspected cult member. Good street knowledge of the city told him where some of these photos were taken, and he didn't need to read the location which had been scribbled on the back of the images. He'd have to watch his step in the entertainment district. It was a far cry from the extravagant theatres and restaurants that filled the upper city's district. Below the towers the entertainment consisted of bars where the booze was cheap and watered down, along with brothels and gambling dens where hard-working men would go to lose their hard-earned cash. Many of them with wives and children at home. It would be in these places that he would look to find some answers.

CHAPTER FIVE

'WEALTHY BIG CORPORATION BOSS FOUND DEAD IN HIS HOME'

The headline of the Smoke City Gazette read.

Harry held the newspaper close to his eyes and read through the article. He was right: the poor dead officer only got a mention towards the end of the story.

"Are you ready to go, Detective?" the lift operator asked. "We will be leaving shortly."

"Yeah." Harry groaned, stubbing out his cigarette on the floor with his shoes.

They were standing inside the precinct's main elevator which led down into the undercity. It was large enough to transport vehicles, supplies and squads of officers to and from the undercity. An armoured police truck containing the district's support unit had pulled up next to him. Inside sat hardened men and women ready to assist with transporting prisoners and quelling any spontaneous bouts of violence which were becoming an almost daily occurrence. The support officers were better equipped than the patrolmen. They wore metal face masks which obscured their identity and made them greatly more intimidating than regular officers. Their torsos and shoulders were protected by leather vests and pads. Each carried a long truncheon, their service revolver and two pairs of chain handcuffs. Secured to the interior walls of the truck were pump action shotguns and heavy metal shields. Harry had only seen them used on a handful of occasions, usually when he was following up a lead and stumbled upon a gang hideout or found himself amid some minor insurrection or food riot.

"Going down!" The lift operator bellowed as he pulled the lever, which was followed by the sounds of metal cogs turning and grinding. The lift jolted sharply and then began to lower slowly. It had been some months since Harry had been in the undercity, and each time he stepped foot onto the cobbled streets he was reminded how good he had it. He pitied its residents, particularly those unfortunate enough to have been born there, with little opportunity to escape unless they could find a job waiting tables for the rich or scrubbing their toilets. And still that wouldn't pay well enough for them to afford a place in the sky. If they were lucky, they may be able to live with their master and be ready to answer their every call and tend to their every need.

Every mayor of Smoke City promised to do more to help the youth of the undercity, to provide them with greater opportunities for better schools and training. This would usually involve a small handful of orphans selected during some press event to be taken above the fog and offered the best future. Little or nothing was reported after their apparent rescue. Nobody really knew what happened to them afterwards. Although Harry assumed Victoria would have been one of these children. She was one of the few who had made it, one of the lucky ones. Even if it did mean a life spent in servitude of her alleged saviour. Several minutes passed, and the lift was still working its way down the building. Harry tapped the revolver which he had moved onto his lower back – he could draw it with his left hand if his .45 ran dry. His semi-automatic sat underneath his left armpit, nestled inside a leather shoulder holster. His left hand then moved into his coat pocket where he began to fiddle with a set of steel chain handcuffs. Getting back to reading the newspaper, he quickly became engrossed in a story detailing how the world had narrowly avoided a global famine.

It was a minor distraction from the day that awaited him.

The armoured truck fired into life like the last lion roaring before it became extinct. The lift must have been reaching its destination. Black smoke shot out of the truck's exhausts, which slowly started to fill the air like a dark mist. The lift came to a stop behind some heavy metal doors.

The elevator operator walked towards another long metal handle and shouted, "Doors opening!" before pulling it downwards. The doors slowly separated, revealing a wall of smoke which quickly cleared. Ahead of them, beyond the door, was the undercity. The truck began to creep forwards, its loud powerful engine revving. Harry and the remaining patrolmen followed it out past a squad of other officers standing guard by the entrance; they were relieved from their post by their colleagues and would soon be finishing their shifts for the day. Harry nodded at the duty sergeant and walked out onto the cobbled street. Streams of smoke escaped the gutters and disappeared into the bustling street.

Dozens of people walked past Harry and paid no attention to the imposing truck exiting the elevator. The sky was dark above him. Sunlight was a rarity in the undercity. The fog above was often too thick and the towering buildings would block most of what did manage to pierce its heavy blanket. Tall glowing streetlamps provided most of the light, along with colourful neon signs that were plentiful outside of the many bars and brothels.

The streets were cramped, the foundations of the tall buildings that stood kilometres above them were covered in graffiti. Most didn't even have entrances into the undercity and there was no way to pierce their hardened concrete walls. The shorter buildings which didn't stand above the sheet of fog were a mixture of apartment blocks, workshops and warehouses. Harry followed the crowd towards the bars where he knew snitches would frequent. The clothes worn by the people were a contrast from the fashion trends in the upper city. Other than Harry, there wasn't a suit or tie to be seen. Folks wore whatever they could get their hands on. Long trench coats, worn boots and fingerless gloves were common. Many sported headwear including flat caps, bowler hats and goggles.

Once he had found his way into the entertainment district, Harry stood and let his eyes scan the signs above the entrances to the bars and brothels. 'The Tap', the letters glowed against the dark wall in a deep neon orange, although the letter A was flickering and on the fritz. It was a dive bar renowned for attracting people who made it their business to know other people's business. Prostitutes loitered by the entrances, hoping to score a customer who was too drunk to know better, or too desperate. They were all thin, wearing small pieces of leather which left little to the imagination. Their stockings were riddled with holes and ladders. One was probably still a teenager and like many, would lie about her age.

The centre of the cobbled streets was taken up by food vendors, selling dried goods. Fresh food was a rare commodity in the undercity. Most of it was either stolen from the towers above or smuggled from the factories or farms from beyond the city limits. Real meat, in particular, was difficult to come by and even Harry struggled to afford it on his salary. Carbohydrate products such as pasta and noodles were popular, with dried vegetables often sprinkled over the top for flavour. Soup and bread could be found almost everywhere and was the go-to meal for the poorest of the city's inhabitants.

Harry tilted his fedora so it sat low on his brow as he made his way towards the entrance. He kept his hands free should he need to slap a pickpocket away which were rife in the district. The prostitutes didn't make him for a cop as he stepped past them. One of them was lit on fumes, her eyes were glazed, and she swayed gently from side to side in a slow rhythm. Another tried to grab his attention with a wave, but he ignored her and walked into the busy bar. Like the detective's office in the precinct, a layer of cigarette smoke lingered which made it challenging to see into the crowd. The stools against the wooden bar were all occupied, though none of the patrons seemed to be talking to one another. They all sat staring into their whisky glasses. Many were smoking, their ashtrays full of cigarette butts. The shelves behind the bar were stocked full of spirits and most likely watered down. The lighting in the bar was dim, which only added to its moody atmosphere. Leather booths, separated by red glass partitions, were fixed against the walls where couples sat laughing and drinking together. A picture phone with a cracked screen was fixed to the wall towards the back of the bar, by the restrooms. In the corner of the room, stood a tall elderly man playing the saxophone; his hat by his feet contained a sprinkling of loose change. Harry wondered if he spent every night here, making his lips sore for chump change, donated by people who probably felt sorrier for him than actually enjoying his music. It was a sombre track, slow, melancholic.

Towards the back of the bar, in a booth, sat a man drinking a bottle of beer. He wore a worn brown leather newsboy hat and an equally worn brown leather coat. Harry slowly made his way towards the booth and could see that he was alone. The man pulled a notebook out of his coat pocket and began to scribble something.

"Working on your haikus again, Joel?" Harry said, taking a seat opposite him.

The man in the hat quickly looked up from his notebook with a startled expression that quickly turned to one of annoyance and resentment. He was a short, wiry man with dark features. His eyebrows were thick and bushy and met in the middle, and Harry suspected he wore the hat all day and night to shield his retreating hairline. He was pale like everyone else in the bar.

"Great, Detective Quinn," Joel said, leaning back against the partition behind him. "You know, every time you speak to me, I or someone else ends up either getting ruffed up or killed. I am just counting the days until it is me."

"Joel, may I remind you that you are paid to provide information to us. You walk amongst the dangerous people of this city; it's the risk you take. Now I am sure you would be keen to earn some notes. You were never one to turn down a handout."

"A handout, is that what you call it? You're right, I do know dangerous people, but today I don't know nothing."

"So you don't know anything about anything?"

"Nothing about nothing."

"So you don't know anything about the murder of Lucius Volster yesterday?"

"Who?"

Harry leant forward and placed his arms on the wooden table.

"Don't play stupid with me, Joel." His tone turned from jovial to stern. "The city wants this case wrapped up and I don't have time for your bullshit. We play these games every time we meet. Besides, a cop was killed and I'm sure his friends wouldn't like it if a rat knew something and didn't want to spill."

"Well…then you know the drill."

"Oh yeah, I know the drill."

Harry took a quick look around the bar, nobody seemed to be paying attention to him, nor to the snitch sat opposite. He grabbed a handful of dollar bills from the inside of his coat pocket and slid them across the table. Joel pulled them underneath, licked his thumb and flicked through the wad of notes with his stubby fingers. He scanned the room before stuffing it into his own jacket pocket.

"Alright, what do you want to know?" said Joel.

"What you know."

"Look, there are talks about this new group on the scene. Call themselves the smoke kids or something."

"Children of the Smoke you mean."

"Yeah, that's them, this lot are a little different from the usual gangs that roam the alleys. They aren't interested in extortion, robberies or slinging fumes. Nobody really knows what they want or where they come from. They all wear these long red capes and have their heads shaved. Real weird shit. Their symbol, which I am sure you have seen, keeps appearing on street corners. They walk around handing out flyers with cryptic messages."

"What sort of messages?"

"Things like, 'defy your overlords' or 'subvert the powers above'."

"Where do they hang out?"

"I don't know."

"I struggle to believe that, Joel."

"I am being serious, I tried to tail one a while back, lost them in a back alley. Stepped through a load of smoke which had come up through the grates. It was like he disappeared into it. Spooky shit, you know."

Joel sat up straight and scanned the bar with his dark, anxious eyes. He was either worried someone was listening in or someone was coming for him.

"How many do you reckon there are?" Harry said.

"Dozens," Joel replied, his eyes locking back on Harry's.

"Where can I find one?"

"They usually hang about in the slums; you know the real slums. The places where people live and sleep in small cages stacked up against the wall."

Harry knew these streets. Not everyone was fortunate enough to be able to afford an apartment. The poorest had to resort to sleeping in these small metal cages, barely fit for an animal. The people there were desperate and would likely be easily coerced or led, especially if there was a promise of a better future. This was where many of the gangs filled their ranks, promising the most vulnerable a future of riches, drink and women. There was supposed to be a greater police presence in these areas to deter this activity, although the cops hated working it due to the bad smell, cramped conditions and risk of being stabbed in the back by an aspiring young gangster who wanted to make a name for themselves.

Harry had been spun enough tales of nonsense in his time. Joel, for all his faults, had never fed him bullshit and had always been reliable. Yet something felt off this time, Joel seemed a little more on edge than usual, like this cult genuinely frightened him.

"Joel. You good?"

"Me, yeah sure. Why?"

"You seem a little…twitchier than usual."

"No, just…oh shit."

"What?"

Something across the room had frightened him. Harry turned and looked over his shoulder to see two stout men in bomber jackets walking towards them. One was bald, wearing aviator glasses. His long ginger beard sat just above his protruding belly. The other was taller, clean-shaven, sporting a buzzcut.

Harry looked back at Joel who had sunk himself into his seat and pulled his hat down, trying to conceal his identity.

The two men stopped at the edge of the table and stared at the quivering wreck of a man. The bearded man leant forward, his gravelly voice was deep. "Joel. Bartholomew wants his money."

"He... he will get it," Joel whimpered.

"When?"

"Soon. I promise."

"You said that last time. Time to pay up, Joel."

"Look. I only got a little on me."

Joel reached into his coat pocket and produced the notes Harry had handed him. The buzzcut leant forward and snatched them out of his hand. Joel quickly withdrew deeper into his seat. Both gangsters inspected the notes before the bearded one looked back at Joel and said, "This aint nearly enough. You are coming with us."

Leaning forward again, the buzzcut grabbed Joel by his jacket and dragged him out of the booth and onto his feet.

"Alright, fellas," Harry said, standing up and stepping out of the booth. "That's enough, let him go."

The goons looked at him, the bearded one sizing his newly acquainted asshole up.

"None of your business, sky dweller, go back up to your fancy tower. Your wife know you're down here?"

Harry didn't reply, he just stared out the two goons. The buzzcut let go of Joel and turned his attention to the defiant man stood opposite him and said, "You can either pay up yourself or join your little friend over here."

"Pay up?" Harry said.

"Yeah. Hand over what you got to my friend right now. You sky dwellers always come with plenty of dough."

"Oh. I only have a little bit on me."

"Well," the bearded man said, "hand it over right now." He extended his arm and opened his palm.

"Ok, one second," Harry said. He reached around behind his back, pretending to go for his wallet. The bearded thug in front of him began to smile. It soon faded when Harry struck him in the face with his revolver. His nose popped and began to bleed all over the wooden table. He staggered backwards, his right hand trying to plug the bleeding. The buzzcut looked at his partner and then turned to see the barrel of the gun stuck in his face.

"Now, give Joel his money back and take a hike. Or you can end up like your friend over there."

The buzzcut didn't move, so Harry cocked the hammer on the revolver.

"Alright, alright," he said, raising his hands in the air. He chucked the bundle of notes on the table and took a step away from Joel. Turning to his wounded friend who had tears in his eyes, he wrapped his arm around his shoulder. The pair quickly scuttled out of the bar. The other customer's eyes were glued to them all the way out the door. The jazzman didn't stop although his tempo seemed to pick up once they left and the other patrons went back to staring at the walls.

Harry de-cocked his revolver and holstered it. "Thanks," Joel said. "I owe you one."

"What was that about? More gambling debts?"

"Something like that. Look, if I hear anything about that cult, the cop or the dead bigwig, I will let you know."

"Good. Now you had better get out of here before they come back with more muscle."

"Good idea. Where are you heading to now?"

"You know where."

"The slums?"

"Yeah, I need to track down one of these cultists, see what they know."

"Good luck, brother, something about them gives me the creeps. I have lived down here all my life, and not much scares me."

"Not even those two goons?"

"No, look, you know what I mean, it's just I don't understand them. I know nothing about them, that sort of thing. And I know a lot about a lot in this town."

"Yeah, Joel, I know what you mean."

CHAPTER SIX

The slums were a complex and often dangerous web of filthy alleyways, tight streets and dead ends. It was the darkest part of the undercity, where the foundations of many towers stood tall. There were no bars in the area, and the brothels were little more than crumbling shacks and tents. Those who were too poor to be able to own their own apartment would find themselves sleeping in metal cages or containers. Some were shared by families; others were shared by groups of fumers who spent most of their day sucking on addictive chemicals through metal pipes and inhalers. When they weren't scoring, they were out stealing and robbing what they could to fund their habit. It was hard to break the addiction since most of the clinics had shut down.

Harry's wife had spent years in the undercity, running these clinics and treatment centres for the addicts. On occasion, when a new mayor or government official wanted to win the hearts of the people, they would throw money at treatments centres and medical products to try and reduce the fume epidemic. None had been successful, and the reports suggested that there were more fumers on the streets now than ever. Many looked down on them, cops would avoid roughing them up as they rarely had the strength to offer much resistance. Their bodies had been wasted away through lack of nutrition and the damage caused by the chemicals. What money they could scrounge went straight on their habit.

The foot traffic picked up as Harry entered the slums, although most of the people kept their heads down and avoided eye contact with one another. Their clothes were even more ragged and worn. Many had tears in their jackets and trousers, some were patched up with different materials. The streets were becoming too narrow for vehicles to drive down. If he wanted support, the cops would have to dismount their trucks and cars, and put their leather boots to good use.

The people who lived here were the poorest in the city. Those who were so poor that they could rarely afford food would rely on soup kitchens and handouts from charities to get by. Harry clocked a couple of guys who belonged to the Junkers, a street gang who liked to attach cogs and gears to their jackets, like some sort of chainmail. They would show off their garish face piercings and tattoos to make themselves more intimidating. When they weren't slinging fumes to addicts, they were teaching kids how to pick pockets and how to handle a blade.

They had a long-standing rivalry with The Black Lungs, a gang who prided themselves on the terrifying mechanical breathing apparatus that they had fixed onto their backs. Almost all of their members suffered with respiratory problems and required these technical monstrosities to breathe. Each wore a face mask that connected to the pumps and muffled their voices which made them sound almost demonic. The Black Lungs were notoriously violent, often using surplus or stolen military equipment to wage war on the Junkers, who they believed were invading their turf. Innocent people were often caught in the crossfire when a shootout erupted. The gangs outnumbered and outgunned the cops who would regularly have to call in the support units in their armoured trucks just to make it a fair fight.

Harry stood in a narrow alley and retrieved a photo from the inside of his jacket pocket. He studied the image which was a photograph of the smokestack. His observation was interrupted by a group of kids who came skipping playfully towards him. He placed his back to the wall and stuffed the photo in his pocket. He had lost wallets and cash before to these nimble and well-trained thieves. The eldest of the group, a thin and malnourished child who was probably about thirteen years old stopped and looked at the detective before shaking his head at the others. The group quickly moved on. Harry pulled out the photograph again and held it out in front of him. He recognised the sign in the photo which read 'PART PLAZA'. It was a junk store down towards the end of the alley. Harry started towards the store and spotted the dirty tin sign on the concrete wall. Next to it, just like in the photo, was the smokestack, crudely painted on the wall. Harry held the photo up and compared the two. He was in the right place. The store was closed; its shutters were down and covered in graffiti. Once he stepped out of the alley, he found himself in a cramped courtyard. An old fountain was situated in the centre, although water hadn't flowed from it in years. It was full of trash and dirt. A young child was working his way through it, trying to find something of use. Several containers and cages were positioned against the walls. A thin elderly man sat inside one with his legs crossed, whose eyes were fixed on the fountain ahead of him. Another child walked past Harry, staring at a piece of paper. The child flipped it over and Harry picked up the smokestack printed on the crumbled sheet. He followed the child who walked towards the old fountain and leant against it. "Hey kid," Harry said softly.

The child looked up at him; his face was pale and covered in dirt. His small fingerless gloves were shabby and falling apart.

"Yes, mister?" the kid said sheepishly.

"You mind letting me look at that paper?"

"Depends."

"Depends on what?" Harry knew where this was going. He reached into his jacket pocket and grabbed a cash note.

The child extended his palm, and Harry slapped a note into his small weak hand. He didn't even bother to check how much he gave him; the kid needed it more than he did. His eyes lit up as he studied the note, and he quickly handed over the piece of paper.

Harry unfolded it; it read:

'FOR THOSE WHO WANT TO SEE WHAT LIES BEYOND THE SMOKE, THROUGH THE GREY SHEET OF FOG. LOOK FOR THIS SYMBOL AND YOU WILL FIND A FUTURE IN THE SUN.'

On the other side of the paper was the symbol, nothing else. There were no address details or contact numbers. It was just a cryptic flyer with a confusing message. Why would anyone want this? Even the poorest child or most desperate fumer would find little use for this.

"Where did you get this from, kid?" Harry said, folding the paper and putting it in his pocket.

"A tall bald man gave it to me."

"Where?"

"In the markets."

"Which ones?"

"Down there." The kid pointed at an alley behind Harry.

"What did he look like? The man who gave it to you."

"I told you; he was tall and bald."

"Anything else?"

"Yeah, he had a long red coat, the funny drawing on the back of the paper was on the back of his head."

"Was he alone?"

"No, there was another tall bald woman with him."

"When did they give this to you?"

"Just now, just before I came back over here."

"Alright, thanks, kid. You mind if I keep it?"

"Sure, I was going to throw it in the fountain anyway and make a wish."

Harry smirked at the sweet kid and then flicked him a coin. He caught it and smiled with joy at the detective before scurrying away.

The market was a mixture of food and junk vendors. People bartered with whatever they had and prices were constantly being haggled. It was a loud, claustrophobic environment where it was almost impossible not to bump shoulders with the person walking next to you. Walking past a meat vendor, Harry's attention was drawn to something on the grill. It was probably a rat or some other unsavoury animal. People were desperate enough to eat just about anything in the slums. Most drew the line at other people and there hadn't been a cannibal case in some time now. The vendors tried to recapture Harry's attention, presenting him with bowls of God knows what and other worthless trinkets which would have some value to someone somewhere. He wasn't interested in tat that day; instead, he scanned the busy crowd trying to spot someone wrapped in a long red robe.

He stood for several minutes before spotting a hooded figure clad all in red. Harry slowly moved towards them, entering the busy crowd again. The figure was walking away from him, back towards the market's exit. He had trouble keeping up with them as the crowd became denser. It was time to push a little harder. Ahead of him were a group of Junkers walking towards the crowd, their rickety, spiky and shiny metal clad coats hanging off them. The hooded person was heading straight for them. A portly man pushed into Harry and spun him around. A small group of Black Lungs appeared from where he had entered the market. Something was about to go down and he needed to get himself and the hooded person out of the impending crossfire. He turned again and spotted the figure still making their way through the crowd. Now having to wade through it and force people out of his way, he knocked an elderly man onto their backside who chastised him before someone helped them up. Harry managed to get within arm's reach of the figure and went for their hood. Grabbing a handful of cloth, he pulled it backwards and was surprised when he recognised the face beneath it.

"Victoria? What are you doing here?" Harry said, confused.

"The same thing you are, detective," Victoria said with a hint of frustration in her voice. She slapped his hand off her clothing and adjusted her hood.

"It's not safe for you to be down here. I am getting you out of here."

"The hell you are, Harry. I have just as much of a right to find out who killed my father as you do."

"I am a cop, Victoria; this is my job, dammit. We need to go, now!"

"Why? What's the matter?"

"I think there is about to be a gang battle."

But before Victoria could respond, a loud crack ripped through the entire market. There was a scream followed by another crack. The crowd began to panic and move towards the exits. Harry looked around to see a Black Lung with a smoking, long-barrelled pistol in his hand. He turned his attention back to the Junkers who drew concealed pistols from their waistbands and took up positions behind the food stalls. They were modified with an assortment of sights, magazines and muzzle breaks.

"We are leaving!" Harry commanded, grabbing Victoria firmly by the arm and pulling her close to him. As he did, he smelt her aroma and heard her whimper. Another crack was heard, this time closer.

Gunfire was exchanged by both gangs, a man in front of Harry was hit by a stray round and fell to the floor. Victoria screamed in fright before being pulled downwards by Harry.

"Stay low and follow me," Harry said, drawing his .45 from his shoulder holster. As he went to move, he saw another figure wearing a long red robe, hiding behind a junk stall. Their head was shaven, and they had a black mark of some kind on their skin above the base of their neck. It had to be a cultist, but Harry now had other priorities. Still, he couldn't just ignore them, he had to try and get close and see what he could find. Bullets began to whizz over their heads as the gang members took cover behind various stalls and fired at one another.

Harry held Victoria tightly with his left hand as they made their way through the crossfire towards the cultist.

"Is that...?" Victoria muttered. The robed figure catching her attention.

"I think so, but right now we just need to get out of here alive," Harry said. He started scanning the market around him.

The crowd had thinned; many had sprinted to the surrounding alleys. Those who remained took cover and crawled out of the firing line. Harry and Victoria kept low as they headed towards the stall ahead of them. The owner had pulled the shutters down, hoping the thin metal would shield them from a stray bullet. As the pair dived behind a nearby stall, a Black Lung stepped out in front of Harry who saw the gun in his hand. Harry heard him gasp from behind his mask as he raised his rusty pistol towards him and Victoria. The detective was quicker, he took a knee, extended his arm and fired twice towards the gang member. The Black Lung screamed a muffled groan before falling backwards onto the ground where he went limp.

"My God, Harry!" Victoria screamed.

"Don't think about it, let's go!" he said.

Harry pulled Victoria past the lifeless body. The cultist continued to take cover by a stall ahead of them. They hadn't noticed the pair yet. Harry spotted another Black Lung take one to the chest before falling to the ground. The remaining two fired as they withdrew back to safety. The Junkers pressed forward, leaving their cover and firing wildly at their rivals.

"Now!" Harry said, pulling Victoria towards the next stall.

They took cover behind a thin wooden wall which would do little to shield them from any stray rounds. About five metres ahead of them was the cultist. The firing stopped and everything became silent. Harry peeked over the top of the wall to see the Junkers pushing forwards away from them. He took his opportunity to get close to the cultist. He let go of Victoria but checked his shoulder to see she was still following closely.

As he stepped forward, the cultist stood up and looked at him. Before Harry could say anything, he heard a robotic, clunking sound followed by several loud thuds. Beyond the cultist he spotted a mechanical bi-pedal machine stomping towards them; its metal legs slamming hard onto the concrete floor beneath it. The rider, a Black Lung was sitting behind an armoured plate. Two large cannons sat atop the plate and began to fire at the Junkers. One took a round to the chest. Cogs from his jacket exploded into the air as he fell backwards. The heavy calibre ripped right through him and carried on through several other flimsy stalls. The Junkers were panicking and firing rapidly at the metal monster that marched towards them in a terrifying fashion. Their rounds ricocheted off the metal plate which protected the rider. Another powerful round ripped through the air and hit a stall next to Harry. Chunks of wood and splinters smashed into himself and Victoria. The cultist threw their hood over their shaven head and turned to make their escape. As they did, a loose round caught them in the back, and they fell forward onto the ground. Paper leaflets escaped their robes and littered the floor around them. Harry crawled towards where they had fallen. Rolling them onto their back, he saw a trail of blood leaking from their mouth.

Harry said. "Why did you kill Lucius Volster?!"

"We...are the children...of..."

"I know what you are. Where are you hiding?!"

"Harry!" Victoria screamed.

He looked up to see the metal walker turn and face him, its destructive guns trained on the three of them. Stretching forward, he grabbed a handful of flyers along with a leather pouch which had fallen out of the cultist's robe. He was relieved when a volley of rounds fired by the Junkers smashed into the walker's metal plate and drew its attention. He looked down at the cultist whose eyes were now shut and her body limp. Victoria grabbed a handful of his coat as she went to stand up. He followed, clutching the pouch and papers in his left hand.

They made their way out of the market, away from the gunfire down a narrow alleyway. Smoke by their feet. Both panting, Harry took a deep breath and said, "Are you ok?"

"I think so," Victoria whispered, gathering her breath and composing herself. She stood up straight and brushed flakes of dust and wood off her long coat.

Harry walked past her, deeper into the alley and said, "We need to get out of here. Come on."

"Wait a minute, Harry, we still don't know anything about the cult nor my father's killer."

"I am hoping whatever is inside this pouch and on these flyers can give me a clue. Right now, I want a stiff drink and to be out of this godforsaken place."

"This godforsaken place was my home once, you know."

"I know, and every time I come down here, I or someone I know ends up hurt, or worse."

"It is worse now than it ever has been. It doesn't help that your colleagues are down here less and less. And the ones that are here are almost entirely uninterested in what goes on."

Harry adjusted his hat and re-holstered his pistol. He stuffed the crumpled pile of paperwork into a pocket and carried the leather pouch in his left hand.

"I don't have time to debate the ethics of police work with you right now. I am leaving the undercity for the day and so should you."

"Fine, but I want to see what is in that pouch."

"Why?"

"Because, Harry, it may lead me to my father's killer."

"You don't need to find them. I do, dammit."

He was getting frustrated with Victoria's persistence now. It was bad enough that she was knocking around the same dangerous streets that he was, but to demand to examine evidence was getting a little obstructive.

"We can argue all day long about my involvement in this, but right now I also want a stiff drink and to put the fucking horrors of what I have just witnessed behind me."

The cursing took Harry by surprise. Victoria had an edge to her. He never figured a woman of her station would voluntarily take herself down into the undercity, let alone deep into the slums. Victoria stared deeply into his brown eyes, refusing to budge on the matter.

"Fine, but we are going straight back to my place," Harry said,

"Fine," Victoria replied, adjusting her coat one final time before walking ahead of the frustrated detective.

CHAPTER SEVEN

t was dark by the time Harry and Victoria made it back to his apartment. They had taken a police elevator back up above the fog. He had reported the shootout in the market to the sector sergeant who didn't seem particularly interested in the incident, nor overly concerned with the welfare of either of them. If anything, it was just another report he had to file before his watch ended.

As Harry unlocked his front door, he chastised himself silently for not tidying the place before he departed that morning. Although, he wasn't expecting company. It was the first time a woman had set foot in his home since his wife had passed. Victoria followed him inside and remained silent.

"Please," Harry said, hanging his hat on a wooden coat rail, "make yourself at home."

Victoria examined the untidy apartment before removing her coat and hanging it next to his hat. She moved some discarded clothing and took a seat on the couch. She sported a pair of grey cargo trousers and a black T-shirt. It was a stark difference from the dress she'd worn during their first encounter.

Harry walked past her and said, "You want a drink? All I got is whisky. Cheap stuff."

"Sure. Thanks," Victoria replied, unlacing her leather boots. She took them off and let them drop onto the wooden floor and rubbed her tired soles.

"I don't have any mixers, so I hope you don't mind it neat."

"Neat is fine. You got any ice?"

"Yeah."

Harry threw a handful of ice cubes into two glasses before pouring the cheap liquor into them. He carried them out of the kitchen and back into the living room where he placed a glass in front of Victoria. He took a sip and let the burning fluid run down his throat which burned like a small fire. Victoria took a greater sip and then placed the glass on the wooden table.

"What was that thing in the market? That mechanical beast," she said.

"I think it was an old army walker. Either they had stolen it or built one from scratch using old blueprints and spare parts."

"Are they common?"

"Not really, although Black Lungs will try to get their hands on anything if it gives them the advantage. They have an affinity for mechanical contraptions; it's like they worship machinery or something."

"I keep seeing those poor people being caught in the crossfire. They weren't a part of it and deserved better."

"That they did," Harry said. He took another sip of liquor before reaching for the leather pouch. He unravelled it to reveal a bunch of documents and inscriptions.

"What is it?" Victoria asked.

"I don't know." Harry spread the paperwork over the table.

Victoria picked up a sheet and examined it.

"Follow the smoke should you wish to embark on a new beginning," Harry mumbled.

"What?"

"Just what is on the sheet." Harry flipped the paper over and showed Victoria.

"Oh. This one…this is a map or something."

"Let me see."

She handed the paper over to Harry who studied it for a couple of seconds. It was a map of a part of the industrial district which surrounded the edges of the city. He placed it back on the table and said, "I think I know where this is."

"Oh yeah?"

"Yeah, it's an abandoned foundry on the outskirts of the city. Had a nasty fire some years ago. The company which owns it keep talking about repairing it and re-opening it, but is always coming up with reasons not to. A lot of people died in the fire."

There was another copy of the map along with a photo of the building. Harry studied it before dropping it back onto his table.

"You don't think this is their hideout, do you?"

"I don't know, but I think I should go check it out."

"You mean we."

"No. I mean I, it's way too dangerous for you to tag along. Besides, you'll just get in my way."

"Get in your way?! If it wasn't for me you'd have probably been killed back in the market."

"You think that's the first time I've been caught in the middle of a shootout?"

"No, of course not. You shot that man dead with little hesitation. It's obvious you… you are ok with that sort of thing."

Harry polished off the rest of his drink and slammed the glass hard on the table.

"I… it is never easy, you know. I…used to be able to remember all of them."

Harry stopped looking at Victoria, his eyes focused on the empty glass on the table.

"I… sorry I didn't mean to…ouch…dammit!"

Harry's gaze returned to Victoria, and he noticed she had a cut on her left arm. Victoria pressed her hand against it and winced.

"Here," Harry said, "let me help." He stood up and went back into the kitchen; a few moments later he returned with an old first aid kit inside a tin box. The cut wasn't deep enough to require a trip to the hospital and all it would take was a little glue. Harry opened the tin box and selected an alcohol wipe.

"This may sting a little," he said as he opened the packet and pressed the wipe against the cut. He heard Victoria gasp gently and shut her eyes.

"Sorry," Harry said, dabbing the wound.

"You think it was from a bullet or something?" Victoria said, opening her eyes and staring into Harry's.

"No, the wound is too clean, I think you were cut ."

"Maybe from all the exploding wood."

"Maybe." Harry poured a small amount of glue into the wound and held it shut for a few seconds. Once the glue had taken, he applied a couple of sterile strips and then wrapped a thin bandage around Victoria's arm. Her skin was soft and delicate.

"Thank you, " Victoria said softly.

"Don't mention it."

"Where is your wife, Harry?"

"She died."

"Oh. I am so sorry. I didn't mean to pry, it is just I assumed you would be married."

"I was. She was killed by a fumer in the undercity a couple of years ago."

"That is awful. How long were you married?"

"Seven years. She was a nurse. Spent a lot of her time running clinics in the undercity. Trying to help those who needed it the most. That's where we met, back when I was a patrol cop during my probation. I used to have to turf out vagabonds and other miscreants who would either be caught trying to steal the supplies or refusing to leave once they had been given their treatment. She used to say I was more patient and kinder than the other cops. That I preferred to talk someone down rather than get physical with them. A lot of good that did me."

"What do you mean?"

"One day, a particularly desperate fumer came in trying to get something to get him through the day. After Caroline had given him his daily dosage, he refused to leave and demanded more. He got angry and smashed up the store. The patrolman who attended roughed him up a bit before slapping a set of cuffs on him. Caroline, in her typically good-natured self, called me and asked if I could have a word with the officer who made the arrest. I spoke to him and managed to convince him to release the fumer. Despite his objections, he let him go on his way. A couple hours later, the fumer returned and robbed the clinic. Caroline tried to stop him taking the strongest of meds, probably because she feared he would overdose on them. The fumer stabbed her seventeen times before disappearing into the night."

Harry closed the lid on the tin box and placed it on the table, next to his empty glass.

"My god, Harry. I… I…" Victoria began to cry. "Did you manage to catch him?"

"Nope, I can only assume he overdosed not long after in some rotten alley somewhere."

"Do you…" Victoria muttered.

"Do you want another drink?" Harry interrupted.

"Oh," Victoria said. "Sure, thanks." She leant forward and downed the rest of her glass.

Harry quickly stood up and retrieved the bottle from the kitchen counter.

After refilling both their glasses, he got to work on examining the leaflet and other documents that littered his table.

"This one is another map. Buildings have been circled," Victoria said as she handed him the piece of paper.

Harry studied it and wondered what the annotations were for. The buildings were a mixture of towers and other grand designs found above the fog. One was The Grand Theatre, which was often seen as the crown jewel of the city. It was a huge and beautifully constructed dome in the centre of the upper city's entertainment district. It regularly housed the finest opera singers and performers this side of the continent.

"I don't know, maybe they are plotting on doing something here. You said yourself they have been involved in damaging infrastructure," Harry said.

"Maybe. Hopefully we can find out more at the factory tomorrow," Victoria said, twisting her arm to look at Harry's handy medical skills that she assumed he had picked up from his dead wife.

"We?"

"Yes, we."

"There is no we. It is way too dangerous. You saw what happened down there," Harry said. He pointed his index finger straight down between his feet. "I can't have you getting hurt, or worse."

"I have a right to find my father's killer. And have I not proven that I can keep up with you?"

"What you've proven is you are incapable of leaving this sort of business to the professionals."

"Professional? Is that what you call it? Sliding bank notes to snitches, grabbing onto a woman you mistook for a suspect, letting your one lead die in a shootout which had nothing to do with them."

Harry leant back onto his couch. She was right: he had been sloppy and had made mistakes. Mistakes that could have cost him the case, or his life if things had gone another way. Victoria was tough, no doubt about it. She stared at him with a kind of ferocity and devotion he hadn't seen in a long time. Shaking her would be hard, and aside from tying her up in his apartment he didn't know how he would convince her to keep away.

"Fine, but if you fall behind, you stay behind," Harry said, standing up. As he did, his picture phone rang. He looked at Victoria and made a gesture with his hand for her to step into the kitchen out of view. Once she was out sight, he lifted the cone off the receiver and an image of a thin elderly man wearing a chauffeur outfit appeared on his screen.

"Detective Quinn?" the elderly man said.

"Yes, who am I speaking to?"

"Apologies for the late call but my boss has only just arrived back in town. You see I work for a Mr Horus Volster, the son of the late Lucius Volster. I believe you are investigating his untimely passing?"

"Yeah. That's right."

"Horus would like to have a private conversation with you. He wishes to consult with the man who will hopefully bring his father's killer to justice. He is willing to fund your investigation and provide resources should you need it."

"I appreciate the offer, but the department has strict rules when it comes to accepting help from outside sources. It can be deemed as favouritism, bordering on corruption. Buy a cop, as the old saying goes."

"I understand your apprehension, but please, if you would rather have this conversation with Mr Volster... ."

"Call me when he is free, we can set something up."

"Well, detective. He is free now, as a matter of fact we are parked on a platform just below your apartment. His time is precious, you see, he will be in meetings for the remainder of the week, trying to stop the vultures from picking the bones clean of his father's company."

Harry sighed, now there were two Volsters who wanted to deal with him directly, and one of them was standing in his damn kitchen.

"Ok," Harry muttered, "give me five minutes."

"Very well," the chauffeur said before ending the call. The screen went black.

Harry turned and looked at Victoria who poked her head around the door frame. "Was that Arthur?" she said.

"Who?" Harry asked, puzzled.

"Arthur, my brother's aide."

"You mean the chauffeur?"

"Yes."

"Then yes, he says your brother is downstairs and wants to talk with me, right now."

"God damn him."

"What?"

"He will try and manipulate the situation, take control of it. Offer his own people in your place or to assist. He will promise you rewards and bonuses if you can wrap this up quickly. Don't fall for any of it – once he has what he wants from you, he will toss you aside."

"A little like you will do I imagine?"

"Don't compare me to him."

"Fine. Look, I need to go down and at least hear what he has to say, if he thinks I will accept his offer, maybe he will leave me alone in the meantime."

"Ok, just don't be a sucker."

Harry pondered those words before heading for the door.

CHAPTER EIGHT

The limousine parked on the platform was an exquisite piece of machinery finished in a pristine white coat along with a polished silver hood ornament. Harry didn't recognise the make but assumed it was some luxury line from overseas that only the most prosperous could afford. Its wheel arches protruded from the rest of its body and partially covered its spotless alloy wheels. The windows were tinted so dark that it was impossible to see inside. Stood by the rear door was Arthur, Horus' aide.

"Detective Quinn," Arthur said, extending his hand and offering a handshake. Harry accepted it and felt a firm grip against his own hand. The old man still had some strength about him. A long scar ran down his right cheek. He had the bearing of a war veteran.

"Please, if you wouldn't mind," Arthur continued, opening the door for Harry to climb inside.

Harry nodded and stepped into the beautiful machine. The interior was made almost entirely of a dark brown leather which was odour-free and well maintained. To the side was a drinks shelf, a bottle of bourbon sat in a decanter next to some empty glasses. Sat opposite him was a young man with slicked-back hair and a thin moustache.

His pinstriped suit probably cost more than what Harry made in a year. He leant forward and extended his hand and smiled.

"Detective Quinn I presume," Horus said.

Harry accepted the handshake and felt another strong grip crush his fingers. He wondered if this was how all Volster men shook hands. Perhaps it was their way of asserting dominance early on, or perhaps Harry had just become delicate as of late.

"Horus Volster," Harry said.

"That is I. It is a pleasure to make your acquaintance."

"Likewise." Harry was partially lying – he didn't really want to be sitting in the back of this car right now, despite how comfortable and luxurious it was.

"Well, you are everything I would imagine a Smoke City detective to be. You look about as tough and as hard boiled as they come."

Horus spoke with a tone fit only for the sleaziest of businessmen. It was a mixture of complimentary yet condescending at the same time. Like he was letting Harry know he was polite but also in control of the conversation.

"There are tougher out there."

"I am sure there are. Now, I know you are a busy man, so I do not plan on taking up too much of your time. I just want to offer my services to you and to assist you in your pursuit of my father's killer."

"What sought of services?"

"Cash, cars, equipment, personnel. You see the Volster company has its own R and D division. We often provide expertise and equipment to the government, including the military. If you are in a jam and your own police department are unable or unwilling to help, I want you to know you can count on me." Horus leant back and placed a cigarette into a long black holder and lit it with a match.

"Apologies, where are my manners," he said. "Would you like one?" Horus reached for a shiny tin and offered the detective a tailormade cigarette. The letters 'HV' had been embroidered on the lid in what appeared to be gold.

"Thanks," Harry said, selecting a cigarette and accepting a light from the still burning match.

Taking a long drag, Harry asked, "What do you want from me?" The blend was rich and flavourful and put his own favoured brand to shame. These certainly weren't something one could buy from a kiosk.

"Just that you keep me in the loop of your findings. And that you bring my father's killer to justice. And if that means bending the rules and requiring my help then so be it."

"I won't break the law for you, Mr Volster."

Horus waved his finger at Harry and smiled. "You see, I like that in a man," he said. "You have boundaries, and you are also respectful to another person. I am not asking you to do anything you are uncomfortable with; however, you strike me as a man with conviction, with honour, willing to get their hands dirty if required."

There it was, Harry thought. The shmoozing and the compliments. The sort of thing which would make a lesser man more obedient and more willing to please.

"I have been told to answer only to my superiors on this one. I am sorry for your loss, and I know how much your father's death will affect the city. But I can't run my own game here, or your game to be precise. I need you to let me do my job and work this case. I appreciate the offer though."

"Very well, detective, just know that I am here if you need me."

Horus leant forward and handed Harry a business card with his contact number and office address on it. It was well made, with tasteful lettering and colouring that put the department's issued ones to shame.

Horus took a long drag through his holder, exhaled and said, "Money talks in this city, detective, I am sure you know that. Needless to say, I am about to become a very powerful man and will be able to open doors to you that were previously locked. You come across something or someone that won't budge. Give me a call."

"I'll be sure to, I promise."

Harry opened the door and stepped back out onto the platform. He nodded at Arthur who was standing like a statue by the front of the limo, before heading back towards the elevator.

Arthur climbed back into the driver's seat and started the elaborate machine.

"Keep an eye on him," Horus said.

Pulling out of the bay towards the lift, Arthur looked into his rear-view mirror at his boss and said, "Yes, sir."

By the time Harry made it back into his apartment, Victoria was curled up on his sofa. She was half asleep. The bottle of whisky was emptier than before he had left. Perhaps today had gotten to her more than she had let on. Afterall, her father had only been dead just over a day, and it was only a few hours ago that she saw several other poor souls gunned down in cold blood.

Maybe Harry was numb to it all. Like all cops, he had become accustomed to violence and the chaos that followed it. He had lost count of the amount of dead bodies he had seen, or times he had pulled the trigger in the line of duty. Harry retrieved some old blankets from a cupboard and gently lowered them over Victoria. His hands brushed against her soft skin again and her thick red hair. She was a beautiful woman, no doubt about it. It perplexed Harry how she hadn't already been married off to a wealthy businessman like some form of hostage negotiation or as part of a trade deal. The weary detective retired to his bedroom and got undressed. As he lay in bed, he thought about the small boy by the fountain back in the undercity, where his parents were and what the future had in store for him. When he finally fell asleep, he dreamt of a lush green field and trees, beyond them a valley with a river flowing through it. Its water cold and crisp.

CHAPTER NINE

Victoria slept soundly through the night. Harry awoke to the smell of coffee and slipped into his bathroom before getting dressed. When he emerged from his bedroom, Victoria stepped out of the kitchen, holding two cups. Despite sleeping on his couch that night, she still looked as beautiful as always.

"Coffee?" she asked.

"Thanks," Harry said, accepting the cup and blowing on it to cool it down.

"I know this may sound rude, but can I use your shower please?"

"Sure, be my guest. The water is still being rationed though. You'll get a powerful few minutes and that'll probably be it."

"That'll be fine."

Harry stepped over to his small television set and flicked it on. The news that morning had a piece on Horus Volster, who stood in front of his company building behind a booth and gave a well-rehearsed speech about the city needing to come together in these trying times and the pursuit of justice. Flashes from a dozen cameras could be heard and seen on the screen. Horus continued on how he had a crack team of investigators pursuing his father's murderer and that it wouldn't be long before the killer was brought to justice. He then swiftly moved on to discussing the company's future and his position in it. Guess that was enough about poor old dad. Harry took another sip of the hot bitter liquid. The shootout in the undercity was only briefly mentioned before the news anchor moved on to another business-related issue.

Harry could hear the shower running so he decided to throw on a new pair of trousers and a shirt. Choosing not to bother with a hat and tie today, not if he was going to be heading out to a derelict foundry somewhere on the city limits. Instead, he selected a long brown leather duster jacket and a sturdier pair of shoes. He slipped another two rounds into the clip of his .45 and slapped it back inside the magazine housing. Once Victoria had finished showering, she slipped back into the clothes she'd worn the day before.

"How is that dressing holding up?" Harry said as he began to inspect it.

"Fine, I think. I tried not to get it wet," Victoria said, cocking her head and raising her arm, secretly enjoying the detective's gentle touch.

"Good, I will bring the first aid kit today just in case."

"I hope we aren't going to need it."

"Me neither. Do you want something to eat before we go? I have some protein waffles somewhere."

Victoria smiled, which made Harry feel stupid. She was probably used to the finest cuisine morning, day and night. Eating meals Harry could only dream of.

"Sure, protein waffles are actually a favourite of mine. But don't tell my brother, or anyone else in the company for that matter."

Once they had eaten, they stepped out of the apartment and Harry locked the door. The drive to the foundry was long and arduous. The pair rode several different highways until they reached the city limits.

"I like your car," Victoria said, observing its ageing yet well-kept interior.

"Thanks. She isn't new, but she is reliable and fast if I need to get somewhere in a hurry."

"It's rare that I sit in the front; I am enjoying it."

"I take it you often ride in those fancy limos that your brother travels in?"

"Oh gosh no. He had that hand built for himself. It's a repulsive machine which only a man like him would choose to ride around in. I prefer a more subtle ride. There are plenty of older, less extravagant cars at the company to use."

"Why the hell am I burning my own damn fuel then?"

Victoria laughed and forced a smirk out of her newfound teammate. The roads slowly took them lower and lower until they were beyond the fog and beyond the undercity. The city itself was surrounded by expansive industrial zones. Most of the manufacturing and production went on in these heavily polluted areas. The sky was always dark. Tall chimneys from the many refineries produced a nearly constant stream of black smoke. Others spurted fire from them like they were a tower inside the deepest circles of hell. The place was woeful and oppressive. Filthy shuttle buses dropped the labourers off outside their workplaces and would collect them at the end of their long shifts. Rusty metal gates surrounded many of the foundries and production plants. Most of the entrances were protected by an overweight security guard, usually an ex-cop topping up their pension. Large metallic monsters, operated by a pilot, would pick up heavy crates and containers and load them onto trucks. These beasts would sometimes come on four legs and resemble an extinct animal found in textbooks or a museum. The pilot would sit towards the front and operate a series of levers and dials to control the mechanical marvel. Thick black plumes of smoke would shoot out of its exhaust ports every time it took a step.

Workplace accidents were common. What little health and safety precautions they had in place were frequently disregarded. Men and women would regularly lose limbs to machinery, suffer nasty burns and some would even be killed. One quick paycheque to the family later and the case would often be settled.

Studying the map, Victoria said, "Not far now, I think,"

They were almost at the end of the zone, beyond them would just be wasteland. The road surface was getting worse, and Harry worried he would suffer a puncture if he kept going. The zone was becoming less and less populated. Most of the factories and buildings in this area were derelict. Many were old and too expensive to maintain, or they had been damaged in 'accidents' and forced to shut. Some of the companies that ran them had long gone bust or been absorbed by the larger, greedier ones. Harry recognised the logo on a wooden sign for The Star Point Organisation which had collapsed when its main production plant was set ablaze and killed a great chunk of its workforce. Many suspected it to be corporate sabotage, and the team of corrupt detectives sent to investigate came up with zero answers. Although it was almost an open secret that they were on the opposition's payroll.

Victoria pointed past Harry and said, "Turn left here."

Harry turned his roadster towards an abandoned foundry. The company sign had been torn down, and its tall gates were locked shut. Its chimney had collapsed a long while ago, and now it was nothing more than a brick stump. Most of the long thin windows had been smashed. The place looked to have been looted many times over.

"You sure this is the place?" Harry said, killing the engine.

"Pretty sure. Look, what is that?"

A dim glow was shining from inside of the brick building. "Somebody is in there for sure. Good spot. Before we go inside, you know how to use one of these?" He produced his .38 revolver and held it in his palm. Two elastic bands were wrapped around the wooden handle which supposedly helped with the shooter's grip.

"A gun?"

"Yeah. In case we get split up."

"I... I mean my father took me to a range a long time ago. But that was to shoot clay discs."

"Ok, let me run it by you, it is very simple. You have six shots, now there is no safety on this thing so be careful around the trigger. It is a double action, so you don't need to cock the hammer every time. Just point, close one eye, line up the front sight in between the rear sight. Squeeze the trigger and don't snatch it."

"O…Ok."

"I am hoping you don't need to use it."

"Me too."

They stepped out of the car and walked towards the rusted gate. The chain and lock around it looked new as if it had been placed there recently.

Victoria lifted the dense padlock and felt its hefty weight in her hand. "I don't think we are getting through that."

"I agree, let's look for another way in."

The metal perimeter fence ran all the way around the foundry yard. About one hundred metres down past the main gate, Harry found a small portion that had been damaged. He managed to bend it enough for Victoria to slip through. She held it open from the other side and Harry followed. His leather jacket snagged on the sharp metal wire, and he thanked himself for wearing it that day as he was out of date on his tetanus shots.

Old metal containers were dotted about the yard. An old bi-pedal walker, leaning on one side where the hydraulics had blown, was stood by a side door. Harry wondered if this was where the gangs had been getting hold of their toys. The piece was ageing and needed some work. But it wouldn't be impossible to get up and running again with a little know-how and patience.

"Harry," Victoria whispered, "this way."

The hinges squealed on a metal door as she pushed it open. She forced it open just enough for them to squeeze through. Harry entered first and then raised his thumb for Victoria to follow. The inside of the foundry was dark and eerie. Large metal crucibles which once contained hot molten metal were now empty and cold. Everything was covered in a black dust. A system of metal walkways ran above their heads and connected to the upper-level offices. Chunks of glass and brick crunched beneath their feet as they walked across the vacant shop floor.

"It's spooky in here, Harry," Victoria muttered. "I can barely see anything."

"Just stick by me. Come on, this way. I think down here was where we saw the glowing,"

They headed towards another metal door, past some withered wooden pallets and other pieces of heavy rusty machinery. Harry pushed it gently and stepped through into a side office. It was long but as bare as the rest of the building. Towards the back wall was a wooden desk, behind it was a noticeboard. They crept through slowly until Harry spotted another faint glow of something coming through the gap in another door by the back wall. He drew his pistol from his shoulder holster and twisted the stiff metal handle, finding the door to be unlocked. Slowly pushing it open, he stepped inside. The glow of a candle partially illuminated the dark room. Beneath it were several pieces of paper. There was a mural on the wall behind it. The smokestack taking up most of it; however, there were other more sinister-looking drawings scribbled beside it. Harry struggled to make them out, one looked like a child crying, the other was a tower up in flames.

"What do you make of this?" Harry said. He turned, expecting to find Victoria behind him but she was nowhere to be seen.

"Victoria?" he said. "Where are you?"

He stepped forward, edging his way back towards the door he had just walked through. As he stepped through it, he felt something heavy smash into his right forearm. It hit him so hard he dropped his pistol onto the floor. He turned to see what it was, but before he could react, he was struck in the back of the head and fell. Desperate not to lose consciousness. Not here in the dark. Where was Victoria and why had he been stupid enough to bring her along? These thoughts quickly faded as he passed out.

CHAPTER TEN

The pain in his arm had subsided, but it was the first thing Harry noticed when he came to. His hands were tied behind his back, but he could still wiggle his fingers, which was a good thing. His arm probably wasn't broken. Whilst he had been out cold, his attacker had removed his jacket and shoulder holster. Looking around the empty room, he saw nothing except the glow of a small lantern in the darkness. Harry checked behind both of his shoulders and found himself tied to a cold metal pipe with cracked dials that ran up the wall.

"Victoria. Are you there?" he grumbled. Nothing. He tried to stand but a bracket which secured the pipe to the wall prevented him from getting any taller than a crouch. Terrible thoughts raced through his mind. Why wasn't she tied up with him? Had they killed her? He told himself to get a grip and figure a way out of here. If she was alive, then he would be her only chance of rescue. There had to be something he could use to cut his binds. The floor was filthy but had been cleared of any debris. All he needed was something sharp. A piece of glass or metal. Beyond the desk where the lantern stood was another metal door. He didn't know where he was in the building. There were no windows or anything that would give him a clue. He rubbed the rope up against the metal pipe, hoping to feel for a snag or something sharp that he could use to sever them. He was out of luck. After contorting his body and arms long enough he began to sweat. It was no use. He gave up after a short while and slumped back to the floor. His attacker hadn't gagged him, but he knew it would be pointless if he tried to call for help. He let his mind race again; he felt like a failure. If he had gotten that poor young woman killed, he would never be able to live with himself. Before he could fall into a downward spiral of doubt and self-loathing, the door to the small room opened. Harry looked to his right to see a cultist standing in the doorway. Like the others, his head was shaven, and he wore their signature red robe. It was secured by a leather belt with a brass clasp.

The cultist stepped into the room and picked up the lantern which swung and shifted the shadows in the room like they had a mind of their own. He stepped forward and squatted in front of the detective. Harry didn't speak, he just stared into the ocean-like blue eyes of the man in front of him.

"Don't be afraid," the cultist said gently. His soft tone inspiring little reassurance. The voice seemed fake, unsettling.

"Where is she?" Harry snapped.

"The girl? She is quite safe, I assure you. Soon you will be reunited. Tell me. What do you want? Why are you here?"

"I am a detective with Smoke City P.D. I am looking into the death of Lucius Volster."

There was little point in lying, they had probably already searched his coat and found his badge and ID.

"Ah yes. Lucius. What a tyrant that man was." The cultist hissed. "His death was only the beginning. We have great things planned for the city. You will soon see, detective."

"What things?"

"Patience. You will have answers soon enough."

"Who are you people? What do you want?"

"You know who we are. We are those who have given all in the name of the smoke. We are the children of this city."

"Bullshit, before you started shaving your head and wearing those ridiculous coats you had a name. You were a normal person. How did a young kid like you get dragged into this freak show?"

The cultist couldn't have been much past his early twenties. He had a youthful look about himself. Freckly with few wrinkles.

"The Leader reached out to me and the others and showed us a future without prejudice, without segregation. And soon, you will see that too if you are willing to accept it into your heart."

The cultist brought both his hands to his chest and smiled at Harry. It was a smile that brought shivers down his spine. Whatever they had planned was going to be bad and Harry knew he had to put a stop to them, but first he had to get out of this room and find Victoria. The cultist stood up and left the lantern next to Harry's feet.

"I will be back soon. And then you will be offered a great opportunity. Although I am unsure if your friend will be offered the same."

Harry stared at the cultist as he walked out of the room and locked the door behind him. 'Great,' Harry said to himself, his inner monologue working hard that day. Even if he could get out of his binds he would still be locked in the room. Still, at least it would give him a fighting chance when his captor came back for him. He had to try something, try and get himself free and prepare himself for what was ahead of him. The lantern was the only source of light in the room. Without it, he would be in complete darkness and that would make things a lot harder for him. He stared at the glowing flame inside the glass box and made his choice. He knocked it over with his boot and then slammed it down onto the glass case. The flame extinguished and the darkness swallowed him entirely. He dragged the chunks of broken glass towards his backside with his feet and stood up as far as he could. He had to be careful not to sit on any of them and cut himself. Lowering himself without his body touching the floor, he felt for something sharp.

The cultist returned a few minutes later and unlocked the door; he was surprised to find the room in total darkness and didn't see the heavy wooden drawer which had been removed from the desk slam into his face. He fell to the floor and was struck again . Harry checked that he was unconscious before patting him down, trying to find something of use. No weapons, although he did find the key to his car. As he stood up, he heard screaming coming from the other end of the building, towards the back. It had to be Victoria, and he had no time to lose. Harry made his way across the building back onto the main floor.

"Unhand me!" Victoria screamed as she was led by two cultists to the centre of the shop floor. Dozens of candles had been lit. A circle of cultists stood in the centre of the room. Inside the circle was a young man on his knees. His hair was greasy and long, and his clothes were riddled with holes and tears. He couldn't have been older then seventeen.

The cultists held Victoria on the edge of the circle. She stared into the eyes of the confused and frightened young man whose eyes darted around the room. A cultist wearing a long gold chain over her red robe stepped onto of a wooden box and raised her arms. The cultists followed except the two holding Victoria still.

"Now, brothers and sisters. We have a new prospect here today. Eager to join our ranks. What is your name?" the woman said.

"Wa...Walter," the young man muttered.

"Walter, tell me, where is your family?"

"Dead...all...dead."

"How?"

"Some through sickness. Some...some were killed in a factory accident."

"And how does this make you feel, young Walter?"

"A...Angry."

"Good. You see, this city is to blame for your family's deaths. Its heart is black and corrupt. And now I offer you an opportunity to be part of a new family, and an opportunity to strike back. Are you willing to take this offer?"

"I guess..."

"Yes? Or no?"

Walter looked around at the ring of cultists stood staring at him. They had all placed their hands into the sleeves of their robes. He was frightened what would happen to him if he said no, but he was also angry. Angry that the city had taken his loved ones from him. He knew he would never have an opportunity to fight back again, never a better opportunity to get his revenge.

"Yes," he said, looking up at the women above him.

"Good. Take a look at the woman behind you. Do you know who she is?"

Walter spun around and stared at Victoria. He saw a frightened young woman being held against her will by these strange people. He pitied her until the cultist began to speak again.

"She is the daughter of one of the most powerful men in the city. His name was Lucius Volster."

"My father used to work for the Volster company, caught an incurable disease from the factory he worked in and died. My family received a pathetic cheque and were forgotten about."

"Then you know yourself that he was the type of man who was responsible for spreading the sickness which killed your father, and many other families. She has played her part for years in the decay of this city and you now have an opportunity to seek some revenge."

Victoria trembled and began to cry but she couldn't speak or move. The cultist stepped off the box and produced a long-curved knife within her robe.

"Take this, Walter, and prove to us you are ready to fight for this city." She slapped the handle of the blade down into Walter's grubby hand.

"What… what do you want me to do?"

"You know what you need to do. That woman right there has kept the likes of you and your family down for years. With people like her running this city, you will never have an opportunity to better yourself, to escape your life of poverty and hardship."

Walter's hands began to shake, and tears formed in his eyes.

"I…I am not a killer. I can't…I am sorry."

He dropped the knife onto the floor and began to sob. Victoria felt a brief sense of relief wash over her, even if it meant she would remain alive for just a few more measly seconds.

"Very well," the cultist said as she picked up the curved knife. Without looking, she swung her arm and slit the boy's throat in one swift motion. He dropped to the ground and pressed his hands against the open wound. He gagged and twitched as the blood escaped his neck onto the dusty floor beneath him. Within seconds Walter stopped twitching and went limp.

Victoria began to panic again. The cultist shuffled towards her and held the bloodied knife out towards her face. Turning her head, she forced her eyes shut as hard as she could. As the cultist pressed the cold metal against her neck Victoria heard a loud bang. When she opened her eyes, she saw the cultists panicking and looking around. The room began to fill with a grey smoke. On the gantry above her was another flash followed by a second loud explosion. The cultist holding the knife fell to the floor and didn't get back up. Her captors let go of her and dived for cover.

She looked down at the dead body by her feet and then felt herself being pulled backwards.

"We need to go! Now!" a familiar voice said.

Victoria spun to see Harry standing behind her. She just nodded and followed him through the smoke, hoping they wouldn't meet the same grizzly end as the teenager behind them. Whoever stood on the gantry continued to fire into the thick bed of grey smoke and covered their retreat. The duo made their way through a set of metal doors until they were back out in the yard again. The firing could still be heard from the inside of the building.

"This way! Come on!" Harry shouted, pulling her arm again.

As they arrived back at the hole in the fence the firing subsided. Harry bent the fence open again and let Victoria through. Once they were both out of the compound, they bolted straight for his car which was still parked near the entrance.

"Do you still have your keys?" Victoria asked.

"Somehow, yeah," Harry said.

Harry pulled his roadster away from the kerb and roared down the road. He planted his foot as hard as he could onto the gas pedal and didn't look back.

After about a mile, Victoria said, "Harry. It's ok, I think we made it."

Harry looked down at the speedometer and eased off the gas a little. Their hearts were still pounding as they slowly made their way back to more populated areas.

"Are you ok?" Harry asked.

Looking at herself in the vanity mirror, she said, "Yeah. I'm…I'm fine,"

"Did they hurt you at all?"

"No, they just dragged me away from you and gagged me. I saw them hit you to the floor. I tried to break free and help you, but I couldn't."

"Who was that throwing smoke bombs and shooting at them from the gantry?"

"I don't know, I thought they would have been a cop like you or something."

"I didn't tell anyone I was down here. Fuck. That was stupid of me. We could have both been killed."

Harry took a sharp right and followed the signs back for the city centre. They would have to cross a toll booth to enter the upper city, and he had lost his credentials. Hopefully, the powerful woman sitting next to him could pull some strings.

"We both made it though. That's the main thing."

"We did, but we still aren't any closer to finding your father's killer," Harry said, tightening his grip on the steering wheel and turning his skin white.

"I don't think that matters now, Harry. I think we need to stop this cult before they hurt anyone else. You saw what they did to that poor young man down there. God knows what else they are capable of doing."

"You're right. This has gotten out of hand."

The radio in Harry's car began to beep. He stared at it for a couple of seconds before accepting the call and lifting the phone off the hook. He flicked a switch on the radio box so only he could hear the transmission.

"Quinn," he answered.

"Harry, it's Chief Carter. I need you down here at the station right away."

"Chief, sir, sorry, now isn't a good time."

"I am not asking you, detective, get down here right now."

"What is this about?"

"Lucius' son has arrived at the station."

"Horus? I spoke to him yesterday."

"No, his other son, Jasper. Oh, and Harry..."

"Yeah?"

"He is one of them."

"I'll be there right away."

He placed the phone back on the receiver and stared at the road ahead of him. "What is it, Harry?" Victoria asked.

CHAPTER ELEVEN

T he door to Harry's apartment was ajar. His guns had been stolen by the cultists, so he had to go in unarmed and pray somebody wasn't waiting on the other side for him. He told Victoria to stay back as he gently pushed it open.

"Hello," he said, taking a small step into his apartment. There was no reply. Paperwork was scattered all over his floor. As he entered his living room, he saw that the rest of his home had been turned upside down. Drawers had been ripped open with their contents emptied. His clothes had been thrown out of the wardrobe and launched onto his bed. Whoever had done this had been thorough. The leather pouch and its contents he had taken from the cultist in the undercity was missing. This had to be the work of someone working for Horus, he thought, as he checked to see what else was missing. They hadn't managed to break into his safe. Not that there was much of value in there anyway. Twisting the dial, he opened it and checked everything was accounted for. He would have to buy himself a new pistol and file a report at the department's armoury to get a new service revolver.

"Who would have done this?" Victoria asked.

"I don't know, but they were a pro. The lock has been picked and the documents we took off the dead cultist are missing. I can only assume whoever saved our asses at the foundry stole the other map and tracked us down."

"Perhaps. Or perhaps they have their own agenda and weren't there for us."

"It's possible. Look, Victoria. I have to get down to the precinct. My chief got hold of me on the way back here. That is somewhere where you can't go."

"I understand. I need to go home and throw on a change of clothing anyway. Once you are done at the station, call me and we can figure out our next move."

"Victoria, it is probably best that you don't tag along anymore. Another couple of seconds back there and you would have been dead like that poor kid. Doesn't the company need you?"

"I know, Harry, but I need to see this through now. They know who I am. Besides, Horus would probably have me do very little now that he is back in town. He will try to keep me out the way or give me petty administrative tasks or something equally mind numbing."

"Fine. You won't take no for an answer, will you?"

"No."

She smiled and then backed away towards the door.

"Call me when you're done, and we can plan our next move."

"I will."

Once Victoria had pulled the door shut behind her, Harry stood in the mess that was his apartment and shut his eyes, hoping the mess would have tidied itself when he reopened them. Sadly, this was not to be. After he had composed himself, he showered and dragged a razor across his face to try and make himself look semi presentable. He threw on the first shirt and tie combination he could find along with some brown slacks and headed to the precinct.

As he stepped through the doors, he saw it was alive with activity and business as usual. Phones rang continuously, cops rushed around the building, and tired, burnt-out detectives scribbled in their notebooks while talking to witnesses at their desk or down the phone.

Harry stood in the middle of the detective bureau amid a haze of cigarette smoke. He spotted Chief Carter in his office who turned around and waggled his finger. Harry didn't bother knocking as he stepped into his office.

"Take a seat, lock the door behind you, Harry," Chief Carter said.

Harry obliged and did what he was asked.

"Damn, Harry, you look like shit. What happened?"

"Where do I start, Chief? I ran into a cultist in the undercity who caught a stray bullet before I could talk to them. Then I tracked down one of their hideouts and nearly got myself killed."

"Slow down. Where was this hideout?"

"An abandoned foundry on the edge of town. I'll point it out to you on a map. You'll find some bodies there for sure. If the other members haven't removed them already."

"Save it. I want it all written up in a report. Leave it on my desk when you are done with it."

"Yes, sir."

"Anyway, there has been some movement. One of the cultists has handed themselves in."

"What? Really? Are they confessing to the Volster murder?"

"Not exactly, but they are offering information on it. The catch is they will only speak to you."

"Me?"

"Yeah, but he won't tell us why. All he is saying is he wants to speak with Detective Quinn."

"You said he gave a name?"

"Yeah, here's the thing, he is claiming to be Jasper Volster. Lucius' estranged drug-addicted son."

"Alright. Where is he?"

"Interview room one. Sergeant Murillo and I will be behind the two-way. If he tries anything we will be in there in seconds."

"Alright, give me an hour to prepare. I need to sort a few things first."

"Take your time."

Harry took his leave. He needed to acquire himself a new badge, ID card and a gun. He was glad Carter didn't ask what he had to sort prior to interrogating his suspect. Losing a gun was always a tricky subject and could result in a disciplinary if the officer was found to be negligent. He would be sure to not to add that he had lent it to a civilian when he filed the report. After acquiring a new badge and ID from administration, he made his way down to the armoury and filled out the necessary paperwork. The armorer didn't ask too many questions before issuing Harry a new piece. Six rounds were popped into the drum before it was stuffed into his holster. Just about ready to tackle the suspect, Harry headed down a narrow hallway towards the interview rooms. They were small, stuffy spaces. The only furniture in them was a desk, a couple of uncomfortable wooden chairs and a dusty recording device. One of the walls had a two-way mirror fixed to it. Those who stood on the other side were able to observe and make notes, spot holes in the suspect's account and give tips to the interviewer on how to dig into them and get them to crack.

Jasper Volster sat upright in his chair, staring at the door in front of him. He barely blinked or moved. His expression was that of a man trying to hold back a smile, despite having a fresh black eye. He seemed almost happy to be there. A shaven head like his fellow cultists, wearing the same robes which were stained with dirt and grime. Nobody had a recent photo of him given that he had disappeared from the limelight some years ago. The one they did have was from an old newspaper article detailing his Saturday night antics in high end nightclubs. But without a doubt it was him. He had the same narrow face.

"He's been like this since we put him in here," said Sergeant Murillo. He stood behind the glass next to Harry and tapped on his leather belt with both of his thumbs.

"What happened to his face?" Harry asked.

"He got aggressive with my guys; they tuned him up a bit."

"Is that really what happened?"

"That's what they told me, detective; I trust my guys. You should as well."

The door opened and Carter stepped into the small room.

"Gentlemen," Carter said. "Harry, are you ready?"

"Yes sir, before I begin. Did he say anything to any of your boys, sergeant?"

"Not much. Just that he wanted to talk to you and that he had answers."

"Was that before or after he got aggressive with them?"

Murillo shrugged his shoulders and turned his gaze back to Jasper, who was sitting still, beyond the glass.

"Alright, let's see what he has to say."

Jasper smiled as Harry opened the door and stepped into the room. His teeth were little more than rotten stumps. Years of fuming had whittled them away. The lips on his gaunt face were permanently scarred from the pipes.

"Detective," Jasper said. "It is a pleasure."

Harry pulled out the chair from the desk and said, "And why is that?"

"Because…you are the one who will help lead this city to its salvation."

"You got the wrong guy, pal. I'm just here to figure out which one of you weirdos iced your old man."

"Ah, my father. Yes, yes. I do not mourn him. Do you know why?"

"Why?"

"Because my father spent his whole life poisoning this city. Killing the people who built it and lining the pockets of those who would look to join him in the clouds."

"Did you do it?"

"Kill my father? No. The Leader wouldn't allow it."

"Is that what you call the guy who runs your little group? Not very original, is it?"

"It isn't meant to be, detective. The Leader does not wish to partake in flamboyant theatrics."

"Could have fooled me with those shaven heads and robes."

"Not all our members dress like this. Only the initiated."

Harry glanced over at the mirror to his left before turning to look back at Jasper.

"What about Reggie, the lift operator. You do him too?"

"Ah, poor Reggie. I had hoped that seeing a familiar face would reassure him. Sadly, he panicked when we explained our offer."

"Is he dead?"

"Oh no, he is quite safe, I assure you."

"What about the cop in the elevator?"

"Casualty in an unjust war I am afraid."

Sergeant Murillo could have stormed into the room and strangled Jasper until the life faded from his eyes. It took every ounce of willpower and self-discipline to restrain himself. Chief Carter glanced over at Murillo and was prepared to step in his way if he made a move, although he doubted he would be able to hold his own against the brute of a man.

Staring at the deranged man in front of him, Harry wondered if years of fuming had destroyed his mind or was he always this sinister? He was sober now though. His eyes weren't glazed nor were his pupils constricted, and he didn't reek of the sickly sweet smell like he had just smoked a dose.

Harry said, "What's your goal, Jasper? What does your cult want? There must be some sort of endgame. You can't keep offing wealthy businessmen, setting fires to factories and spraying alleys with your little logos."

"Oh, detective, we were simply spreading the word and letting people know who their saviours will be."

"Did you come here to be cryptic with me, or do you actually have something to tell me?"

"Of course."

"Good, hold that thought."

Harry flicked the switch on the recording device and typed the date, time and interviewee details using the metal keyboard. A black disc began to spin, indicating to Harry that it was recording.

"Oh, you won't need that. I simply want to give you an opportunity."

"What kind? Tell me?"

"Come closer and I will."

"No chance."

"Then I must remain silent."

Harry hit pause on the machine and left the room. He stuck his head into the room next door and looked at Chief Carter.

"Do as he says, kill the machine. We will record it from in here," Carter said, knowing that it risked being inadmissible in a court of law.

Harry stepped back into the interview room and left the machine on pause. Jasper looked over to his right at the two-way. Murillo felt a chill run down his spine as Jasper stared directly into his eyes. How did he know where he was standing? He took a step backwards, unsettled by the gaze of the fanatic. Even Carter was perplexed by how Jasper had zoned in on the uniform stood beside him.

"Jasper," Harry said, "what have you got to say to me?"

Jasper slowly turned his attention back to Harry and smiled.

"Come closer," he whispered as he leant forward.

Harry sighed silently to himself and prayed he would leave this room with his ears still attached to his head. He did what the deranged man sitting opposite him asked.

"Proctor's Farm," Jasper whispered. "Far out to the east, beyond the city, near the town of Bonesville. The Leader will be waiting for you. Travel alone. Do not bring any other police officers with you. There, you will find your answers."

Harry leant back into his seat. He hadn't heard of the place and didn't have a clue what he would find all the way out in the dustbowl.

"That's it. A location, why did you have to come here to tell me this?"

"Because, detective, I believe you will keep the location to yourself. You see, I am trusting that you travel there alone and do so quickly. If I were to send you a letter or pass a message, I couldn't be sure that it would remain a secret."

"Why me? Why not some other poor cop? I am hardly the most qualified person in this place."

"You are a troubled man, and you may find some answers."

"What kind of answers?"

"Like who killed your wife. And where they are now."

Harry gripped the edge of the table with both hands. How did he know about his wife's death, and how did he know that it was still technically unresolved?

"What do you know about my wife's death, Jasper?"

"Go to the place I have told you to go."

"Tell me now, dammit!"

The enraged detective lunged forward and grabbed hold of Jasper's heavy robe. Jasper didn't try to defend himself or fight back. Instead, he began to laugh and applaud the raging man . Carter and Murillo stepped into the room and pulled him away from the cultist.

"Such fire! Such passion. The Leader will be so pleased when he finally meets you," Jasper shouted, continuing to clap and laugh hysterically.

"That's enough, Harry!" Carter commanded. "Sergeant, take this man back to his cell. Now!"

Dragging Jasper out of his chair, Murillo said, "On your feet, freak." Carter walked Harry out of the room, who shrugged his superior free and held up his hands to show he was calm.

Murillo dragged the still clapping Jasper the opposite way down the hallway towards the cells.

Lowering his tempo, Carter said, "You ok?"

"I'm good, I'm good. It's just this case is getting worse by the day. This isn't your typical angry lover, or bitter wife did it sort of job."

"No. It isn't. I am going to send a taskforce down to the undercity and start rounding up these cultists. The sooner they are off the streets the better. I don't give a damn about budgets or what the commissioner says."

"I don't think that'll be enough. You heard Jasper, he said only the initiated dress like him. What about all the others we don't know about?"

"Well let's hope they aren't privy to whatever the others are planning. I hope that without the key players or these initiated, they will give up this bizarre plan of theirs and lose interest. What did he tell you in there?"

"He gave me a location."

"Where?"

"I can't tell you. He said I had to go alone if I wanted answers."

"Screw that, Harry, it's too dangerous."

"It is, and there is another problem."

"What's that?"

"The location is beyond the city limits. We won't have jurisdiction out there."

"Damn, you need me to get the feds involved?"

"No, they will ask too many questions and take too long. Let me go, David. Let me go and see what is out there."

"Fine. But you'll go as a civilian, that badge won't get you anywhere out in the wild. Take what you need from the quartermaster and the armourer. Find some answers and look after yourself."

"Thanks. I'll let you know if I come up with anything."

"Good, skip the report and head out as soon as you can."

Harry requested a variety of equipment including a leather cuirass from the quartermaster similar to the ones that the support units wore. He also signed out a lever action shotgun along with a box of shells from the armourer. As he stepped onto the car platform, carrying his gear back to his car, he eyed Horus Volster and his aide walking towards him.

"Ah, Detective, just the man I wanted to see," Horus said.

"I am sorry, Mr Volster, as you can probably see I am in the middle of something."

Horus stared at the armour and shotgun in the detective's hand and nodded.

"Yes, I can see that. I told you to contact me should you need better supplies. I have access to the latest military grade equipment, you know."

"What the hell do you want, Horus?"

Horus, a little taken back by Harry's directness, stood himself upright and said, "Ok, I understand my brother is currently in your custody. I would like to post his bail. I want to bring him back into the family now that our father is gone."

"You'll need to make your representation to the desk sergeant. He can advise you from there."

"Thank you. Tell me: where are you going with all that equipment?"

"Out of town?"

"Leaving today?"

"Probably as soon as I can."

"I see. Where are you going?"

"I can't tell you. Police business."

"I see. My offer still stands, detective, if you need anything all you need to do is ask."

Harry just nodded and then walked towards his car. The last he saw of Horus and his aide was the pair entering the precinct.

By the time he got home, it was late afternoon and too long in the day to head out of the city. He unfolded his map and traced his finger along the single road until he saw the town of Bonesville. What an ominous name, he thought, circling the town with a pen. Proctor's Farm wasn't on the map, and he hoped the town's inhabitants would be able to point him in the right direction. He would have to touch base with the local sheriff out there and let him know who he was and what he was doing in his backyard . It would take the best part of a day's solid driving to reach the town. That was without any hiccups such as a flat tyre or weather problems. If they were to get caught in a dust storm, they would have to find shelter somewhere and wait it out.

A voice from the doorway gently said his name. Harry dropped the map and reached for his revolver.

"Harry, it's me, Victoria."

"Dammit, Victoria. You scared the life out of me."

"I am sorry, the door was open."

She stepped into his apartment and pushed the door shut. Harry could smell her sweet perfume from his couch. She had freshened up and wore a long black coat and carried a leather rucksack along with a black travel bag.

"Shit. Sorry, I had my hands full when I came in. I must have forgotten to close it."

"What happened today?"

"I…I met your brother."

"Horus? I thought you met him yesterday."

"No. I mean I met your other brother, Jasper."

"You're kidding."

"No…he…he is with them now."

"Who? The Children?"

"Yeah. Head's shaven, wearing the robe and everything."

"He always was a follower. A sheep. Didn't take much convincing for him to start fuming. I haven't seen him in years. And to be honest, I am in no rush to. Tell me, did he kill our father?"

"No, he said his so-called leader prohibited it."

"Right. What else did he tell you?"

"He told me to drive to a farm, way outta town. There I would find some answers. But I have to go alone. No other cops."

"You know it's probably a trap, right."

"Probably which is why I would insist that you didn't come, but I know you would convince me otherwise."

"You're damn right I would."

"He told me something else."

"What?"

"That I would find Caroline's killer there. Or at least find out his whereabouts."

"Do you believe them?"

Harry stood up and walked towards Victoria. He stood close to her and said, "I do, how would your brother know about my wife? I doubt he read it in the obituary section in the newspaper all those years ago."

"I doubt it as well."

"Where is this farm?"

"About a day's drive east."

"Good thing I brought some provisions then."

Harry smirked at the beautiful woman in his living room.

"Go home, Victoria, I will pick you up at eight."

"I don't want to be all alone in that tower, Harry."

Victoria grabbed hold of his arm gently and took a step forward. Harry stared into her deep green eyes and felt her lips close in on his. Her lips were as soft as her skin, and she kissed him with a ferocious passion he hadn't felt in years. He kissed her back, grabbing hold of her waist and pulling her close to him. Victoria's hands crept up to his chest and began to unbutton his shirt. She traced the hair on his chest and felt his strong shoulders. Harry's lips moved down to her neck as his hands grabbed hold of her buttocks. Lifting her up, she wrapped her legs around his waist. They kissed each other all the way to the bedroom where they collapsed onto the bed. Victoria shut her eyes and moaned gently as Harry unbuttoned her silk blouse and kissed down her body. They made love as a blimp flew past the window; its spotlight illuminated the bedroom. Harry looked up at Victoria, the blinding light made her look like an angel sent down to give him another chance of happiness. Once Victoria had fallen asleep in his arms, he thought about the journey ahead of them. He quickly told himself to stop and enjoy the moment, and for once allow himself to finally be happy, even if it wouldn't last.

CHAPTER TWELVE

Victoria stood by the door wearing a set of grey cargo trousers that had been tucked into a pair of black combat boots. The black leather jacket she wore looked both fashionable and practical. She had braided her hair in preparation for the long trip into the dustbowl which surrounded the city for miles. Harry stepped into his living room and found her trying on his collection of fedoras.

"They look better on you than they do on me."

She turned and smiled at him and tilted the black hat on her head, so it covered her left eye.

"I like your coat. Makes you look like a real adventurer," she said.

Harry had chosen a tan bomber jacket with a fleece lining along with brown cargo trousers and a set of sturdy boots. His leather cuirass sat beneath his jacket, above a white shirt. He had a satchel slung under his jacket. Several bullets were visible on his belt and his holster sat against the right side of his hip.

"You ready to go?" Harry asked.

"Ready when you are."

"I actually have a bit of a favour to ask."

"Go on."

"I am a little worried that my car won't fare well outside of the city limits. The roads out there are treacherous, and I don't think my roadster will make the trip there and back. Horus promised me access to Volster tech, that offer still stand with you?"

"I think we can find something."

Victoria directed Harry to Volster Tower. He parked his roadster on a platform, between two brand new convertibles. The building was brimming with business types. Men and women dressed in expensive suits all rushing around. Almost every man carried a briefcase and had a worn, frustrated look on their face. The women had all kept up with the latest fashion trends, their skirts and blazers looked expensive and straight out of the latest lifestyle magazines. Keeping close, he followed her down a long hallway towards a set of heavy metal doors where she inserted a key into the lock and pushed them open. Beyond the heavy door was an enormous room full of vehicles. Some were hidden under cloth sheets. Harry recognised a couple of models but was perplexed by the others. Sleek looking sports cars and limousines took up most of the room. Some were half finished, missing body panels and wheels.

"What is this place?" Harry said.

"Horus' private collection," Victoria said, turning and smiling at the impressed detective.

"Will he mind?"

"I doubt it, he probably has other things on his mind right now; besides, you said he had promised you resources."

"That he did."

"Here, follow me. I think you will like this one."

Victoria pulled a sheet to reveal a metallic grey car. It sported large tyres with thick treads. The car had been raised so it sat high off the ground. The bonnet was long and curved, concealing what Harry assumed was a powerful engine. It was a four door, with the rear doors opening towards the centre of the car. Four heavily polished exhaust ports stuck out the side of the vehicle. It was curvaceous and looked well-constructed. Not a spec of dirt was present, and it had been buffed so highly that Harry could almost make out his reflection in the paintwork.

"What is this?" Harry asked, rubbing his hand over the bodywork.

"A concept the company was working on. The idea was to create a multi-terrain vehicle that could be used beyond the city limits."

"Who would want that? Nobody leaves the city unless it is by air?"

"Exactly why they didn't persevere with it. It works though, go ahead, it's unlocked, the key is in the sun visor."

With one twist of the key, the engine came alive which sounded powerful and frightening. Harry pressed the gas pedal twice and revelled in the sound of its mighty growl.

Speaking over the noise of the grumbling engine, Victoria bellowed, "Six litre V8!"

Harry switched it off and dropped his arm over the driver's door, a childish grin on his face.

"Won't it drink fuel?"

"Sure, if you floor it. We can load spare jerry cans on the back should we not be able to fill up on the road."

Harry loaded a couple of days' worth of provisions into the trunk of the beast. Protein paste, nuts and other dried goods should they not be able to find a diner on the road. He filled four canteens full of water and handed one to Victoria. The others were placed into the trunk along with their travel bags. The shotgun was placed between the rear and front seats for easy access in case of an emergency. There were rumours that raiders were becoming more common on the highways, and the sheriff departments along with the other law enforcement agencies were struggling to combat them. His satchel contained a handful of spare shells, a flick knife, a set of chain cuffs as well as a leather sap.

"I hope you don't mind, Harry; I asked Arthur to loan me this," Victoria said, presenting him with a small nickel-plated semi-automatic pistol. It was the right size for her petite hands and could be easily concealed if necessary.

"Not at all. You need me to run you through how to use it?"

"No, Arthur took me through it last night. But if I need any pointers I will ask."

"What is his deal anyway? He seems more than just your average chauffeur."

"Arthur? Arthur has worked for my family for years. Before that, I think he may have been special forces. That's where he got the scar on his face. He isn't as old as you might think."

"Figures, he probably had a hard time in his youth."

"He doesn't talk about it much. But he has proven himself more than capable many times. A mad man tried to gun down my father during a press conference once. Arthur disarmed and restrained him in front of all the cameras and press. The police were dumbfounded how a slender old man had done what it would have taken four of them to do."

"What does he think of your brother? Horus, I mean."

"I wouldn't know, you'd have to ask Arthur."

Once they had finished loading the car, they hit the road and headed east. It took them almost two hours to exit the city limits. They would see the humungous towers and buildings in the car's mirrors for many miles, standing dominant above the rest of the city. Once they had travelled beyond the dark, polluted industrial zones, the air began to feel cleaner. Although the sky above them was still grey, like the terrain. Jagged rocks, ash-coloured hills and barren fields were as far and wide as the eye could see. The highway was long and endless. The traffic now mainly consisted of giant road trains pulled by powerful trucks. The cabs themselves were armoured, and the drivers were often armed. Some had tally marks painted or scratched into their bodywork like a bomber plane. Probably for every raider they rammed off the road or sent to their deaths in a ball of iron and fire.

The land around them was bleak and depressing. There were still farms in the country, where the likes of wheat, corn, rice and barley were cultivated. But they were way beyond the cities and protected by armed guards. These goods were exported across the country to the major population areas. After the war, there was a real and severe threat of mass famine. Ginormous underground greenhouses were constructed. Layers of vegetables and plants were stacked on top of each other all the way up to the high ceilings. Indoor livestock farms also became common. Animals were reared in poor conditions and slaughtered as soon as they were able to produce enough meat, which was still expensive for the average person to consume regularly. Most of the city's inhabitants were vegetarians and lived on a diet of cheap carbohydrates, dried vegetables, vitamin supplements, protein pastes and partially filtered water.

Harry enjoyed the sound of the V8 and wasn't even bothered when he lost radio reception the further he got from the city.

"We should reach the town of Bonesville in nine hours with a little luck. We can take turns driving if you want," Victoria said.

"Alright."

"What do you think we are going to find out here?"

"Answers, hopefully. I want to know what this cult have planned. What their endgame is."

There wasn't much to see as they cruised down the straight road which was worn and full of potholes. Harry was grateful for the larger tyres and greater ride height. His roadster would not have lasted out here. Victoria had shut her eyes and lowered her back rest. She had tilted Harry's black fedora, so it covered her eyes. He took his eyes off the road and glanced at her. He wondered if she would still be around after all this was over. His attention was drawn to her a second too long as the car drifted into the dirt beside the road and started to vibrate. Harry hit a deep pothole and quickly corrected his road position, turning his attention back to the endless black line ahead of him.

"You want me to drive?" Victoria said, not opening her eyes or moving the hat off her face.

"No, sorry. Just a lapse of concentration, that's all."

"Uh huh. Just let me know when you want to swap, detective."

Harry smiled but remained focused on the road ahead of him. His thoughts then drifted to the case and how ridiculous it had become. Most murders in the towers were often domestic-related, committed by the bitter housewife, upset when they found out about their husband's mistress. Others were committed by gangsters, who felt obliged to take action when their corrupt wealthy business partner didn't hold up to their end of the bargain. Harry couldn't ever recall a case this insane. Certainly not while he had been on the job.

Four hours passed, and they were approaching a gas station. Not wanting to pass the opportunity to refuel, Harry pulled into the forecourt and was met by a young boy who scurried out of the store to admire the unique and exciting noisy car.

"Geez, mister, what car is this?" the boy asked enthusiastically.

He couldn't have been more than eleven years old; he wore a set of denim dungarees, and a small set of racing goggles were strapped to his forehead. He was slim, but a little more tanned than the other children Harry came across. Despite what seemed like constant cloud cover, he probably got more sun in a month than the kids in the undercity got in their whole lives.

Harry stepped out of the car, stretched his arms out and said, "I don't actually know. What is it called?"

Victoria smiled at the boy and said, "It doesn't actually have a name, we just call it 'The Beast'."

The boy smiled back and then blushed when he saw Victoria walking towards him – he probably fancied her just as much as Harry did.

"You mind filling her up, kid?" Harry said.

"Sure!" The kid grabbed a nozzle and stuck it into the fuel tank.

Victoria kept the boy company as Harry stepped into the small store. Behind the till was a man who Harry assumed was the boy's father. The store was reasonably well supplied, spare vehicle parts, dried foods and even a couple of candy bars were on the shelves. Cigarettes and liquor were behind the counter. Harry figured there was also a shotgun beneath it , fixed with some wire ready to be pulled on a would-be highwayman.

"Howdy," the man said.

"Hi."

"Where you folk heading to? Rarely see cars and couples come through here. Usually just trucks."

"Bonesville, we uh… have some business out there."

"In Bonesville? Must be some strange business for you to have to head out there."

Harry grabbed two sticks of protein jerky from a glass jar and fingered through a wad of cash.

Handing over several notes, he asked, "Is there a sheriff's office in Bonesville?"

"Sure, SheriffMiles. He covers most of this zone."

"You ever have any problems with raiders around here?"

"Not here no, they don't come out this far. You go beyond Bonesville, and you may run the risk. You got protection?"

Harry pulled his jacket away from his hip and presented the man with his leather holster.

"Hmm, you may need a little more than that six-shooter. You got anything bigger?"

"We'll be fine."

"Alright, just watch yourself out there. They'll enjoy picking your fancy motor to pieces and the clothes off your dead bodies."

The young boy scampered back into the shack, smiling at his father.

"She's beautiful," he said gleefully.

"The car or the woman, son?" his father asked.

The boy giggled and then scurried away towards the rear of the store. Harry nodded and thanked the man before heading back to the car.

Victoria was sitting in the driver's seat, she leant out of the window and said, "Figured I had better drive until we get to Bonesville. Given that you nearly killed us back there."

"Yeah alright, be my guest. My time for a little shut eye," He handed her a jerky stick which she bit into and ripped a chunk out of.

Sleeping for a couple hours, suffering from strange dreams until the radio woke him.

"What was that?" he asked, rubbing his eyes.

Victoria twisted a dial and said, "The radio occasionally picks up snippets of broadcasts from random stations. Some are in a different languages and the music they play is like something alien."

"Could it be alien… We are out in the dustbowl after all?"

Victoria smiled and gently swatted at Harry with her hand. They were only a couple hours away from Bonesville now. They spent the rest of the time talking about Victoria's upbringing, how at a very young age, she had been adopted by Lucius and taken from the undercity. She was given the finest education and encouraged to pursue the finest arts and sports. She enjoyed dancing and fencing and regularly put her stepbrothers to shame with a sword. Harry asked about Lucius, what sort of man he was and how he had treated her way up in the clouds. She said he was a stern and serious man and not particularly affectionate to her, nor his biological children. His wife had passed away during Jasper's birth, and Victoria believed he harboured some resentment towards his children. She had been desperate for a girl, so Lucius tried to honour this wish by adopting one and bringing them to live with him and his boys.

Victoria was acutely aware of the problems in the undercity and had spent much of her adult life as a philanthropist, doing what she could to improve the lives of its inhabitants. Jasper and Horus would often tease her about her efforts, saying she should be focused on her future in the towers and not on her past in the slums. They saw anything below the fog as a slum, and often refused to go down unless it was for some corporate photoshoot their father had insisted on. They failed to see that the undercity had its own vibrant culture such as music and art. Some folk were even proud to live there and would look down on the tower dwellers whenever they made an appearance with their tailored suits and polished shoes.

Harry asked how Jasper had ended up addicted to fumes. She explained how he had always been easily led, which probably explained why he was a cultist. Jasper had tried just about every addictive substance known to man, and despite being aware of the acute dangers of fuming, went for it and quickly became addicted in his early twenties. He told her it made him see the world from an outside perspective, that it opened his mind to things he wouldn't usually be able to comprehend. Colours and sounds were so much more vibrant and impactful. The experiences he felt were like no other substance, and when the effects wore off, the world seemed so stale and depressing. He had insisted that Victoria try it, but she refused every time and had to get physical with him once when he tried to shove a pipe into her mouth. She had clawed his face and left three long scratches down his right cheek.

It didn't take long for Jasper to become reliant on the drug and spend most of his days fuming. His father had tried to send him to a rehab clinic and keep the whole affair a secret. But Jasper refused the treatment, and one day decided to pack up and leave for the undercity. He would collect the cheques his father sent to him. Horus would try and convince him to stop, but Victoria suspected Lucius felt like he had failed his son, and this was what their mother would have wanted.

When Victoria had felt like she had talked enough, she asked Harry about his previous cases. What weird and wonderful things he had seen and heard while being a homicide detective in Smoke City. He had humoured her requests with stories about crazy delinquents in both the undercity and the towers. He told her one story about a scorned wife who found out about her lawyer husband's mistress and tried to poison him. Only that she was such a drunk that she poisoned the wrong dish and ended up dying at the dinner table in front of him. He then told her about a killer in the undercity dubbed 'The Sax Slasher' who targeted jazz players after they left the bars. He never stole their earnings, but he would kill them and slash their saxophone into two pieces. It turns out he was a fumer, and whenever he got high he believed the sound of a sax was the sound of the devil, and that it was his mission to destroy anyone and anything that was capable of making it . Harry had brought a renowned sax player on board to help with a sting and had advertised his gig heavily, posting flyers on walls and stapling them to lampposts and food vendors. Once the gig had finished, Harry swapped clothes with the musician and waited in the alley behind the club. As expected, The Sax Slasher approached him and was surprised when he was beaten to the floor by a detective using a leather sap.

Victoria said she remembered reading about the case in the paper and recollected seeing Harry's name. The papers dubbed Harry 'The Dixie Detective', a nod to Dixieland Jazz, which was considered to be the first true type of jazz music.

The time passed quickly, and they were only a couple of miles away from their destination now. It would soon be nighttime, and neither really wanted to be travelling in the dark. Although Harry wanted to try out the powerful spotlights fixed to the front of the powerful car. The pair eventually noticed a sign saying 'Welcome to Bonesville, Population - 672'.

"Wow, small place," Victoria said. "We could fit the entire town into a tower and still have a huge amount of room to spare."

"Yeah, this place is sparse," Harry said, eyeing the short buildings in the distance.

The town of Bonesville was laid out in a grid pattern. The main road ran through the town and was broken up by several junctions. The sheriff's office was in the centre of the town. Most of the buildings didn't exceed three storeys, and were basic in their design. They were mainly flat roofed, and simplistic compared to the striking architecture Harry was used to seeing. This was a town built for a purpose, probably for farming although Harry hadn't seen any around the town when they arrived. Most of the stores had vending machines on the outside, some seemed to be empty or broken. The town's occupants poked their heads out of windows or stepped outside to get a look at the bizarre machine cruising down their streets. They would have been used to seeing large trucks, towing their cargo. But a car like this would be a sight, and not only because it was one of a kind.

As they drove towards the entrance to the sheriff's office, a tall man wearing a hat with a wide flat brim and a dented crown stepped out to greet them. On his feet were what looked like snakeskin boots, with his tan trousers tucked into them. His shirt was bulging at the belly and a size too small for him. A hefty gold star was pinned to his breast. He was clean shaven, with grey eyebrows and dark brown eyes.

Victoria pulled up by the kerb and killed the grumbling engine. Harry climbed out of the vehicle and walked towards the sheriff who took three steps and extended his hand.

"Detective Quinn, I presume?" the sheriff said.

"Yes, pleased to meet you, Sheriff…" Harry said.

The sheriff's handshake was firm but not as overpowering as Horus'. His hand was dry and abrasive.

"Sheriff Miles, but please, call me John. Your office called ahead and notified me of your arrival. A Chief Carter I think he said his name was."

The sheriff's accent was thick and unusual. He dragged out the last word of each sentence and spoke slowly.

"Yes," Harry said. "This is my technical consultant, Victoria Volster. Did he tell you the nature of our journey?"

"Charmed, ma'am." The sheriff tipped his hat at Victoria before continuing. "Only that you had a lead on a case that you wanted to follow up on. But please tell me, detective, what brings you all the way out of the big city to our small town?"

"We are investigating a murder, one of our suspects gave us a location and told us we would find answers there."

"I see," Sheriff Miles said, rubbing his chin. "You had better come inside then. Folk will be listening in."

Victoria looked over her shoulder; many of the townsfolk were leaning out of their windows or stood on the pavement. The children hid behind their parents' legs and peeked through the gap at the strangers.

CHAPTER THIRTEEN

They followed the Sheriff into the building which was sparsely decorated. A desk sat against the back wall with two smaller ones on the opposite side of the room. A pair of cells were fixed by the right-hand wall but were empty. The young deputy sat with his feet up on the table and was reading a magazine about the latest guns and military technology. On the wall behind him was a map of the zone with drawing pins stuck on various points. A fan rotated above their heads, circulating cool air.

"Boy, what have I told you about putting your feet up on the table, dammit!" SheriffMiles shouted at the deputy. "Stand up, we have guests."

The deputy quickly lifted his feet and stuffed the magazine into the desk. He stood up, patted his uniform down with his hands and nodded at the pair. Victoria smiled at the deputy who did the same and then quickly looked away, not wanting to blush in front of the attractive stranger stood in front of him. Harry noticed the deputy's embarrassment and smiled to himself.

"Please," said Miles, "grab yourself a seat and let's get down to business."

"If you don't mind, Sheriff, I would like to stand for a bit. We have been driving for hours," Harry said.

"Likewise," Victoria said.

"Fine by me."

The sheriff remained standing, not wanting to be rude in front of his guests.

"Where is it you folk are heading to then?" he asked.

"Proctor's Farm," Harry said.

The sheriff and deputy glanced at each other with a concerned look.

"Why there?"

"I don't know. I interviewed a suspect, and he said I would find answers out there. You see, there is something going on in Smoke City, a dangerous new cult with a fondness for red robes have been murdering people and sabotaging buildings."

"Red robes, you say?"

"Yeah, and shaved heads. Some have tattoos on the back of them."

"Of what?"

"Of this," Victoria said, unfolding a piece of paper with a smokestack on and placing it on the sheriff's table.

He picked it up and inspected it.

"Strange," the sheriff said, "real strange."

"It is, even for the city's standards."

"Well. Proctor's Farm is a little further out; the problem is it's raider territory and well…there is nothing there."

"What do you mean?" Harry asked.

"It used to be a cattle farm years ago. But then the war happened, and the soil went bad. They tried their hands at those new techniques or indoor growing, but struggled with the infrastructure, power and water supply, those sort of things. They toyed with the underground stuff but couldn't get it to work. Then one day, the family just upped and left. Place is totally abandoned."

"What's there now?"

"Nothing, just some shells of the old buildings – raiders and scavengers have pretty much picked them clean. Though, come to mention it. There have been reports from long haulers and truckers about seeing those people you mentioned on the road or travelling together in convoys. One came through a few days ago and said he saw a woman with a shaved head just stood on the roadside. He thought it was strange as she was alone and looked like she was waiting for someone to pick her up."

"You haven't seen any of these people, have you?"

"No, the work in the town keeps us pretty busy. It may be small, but we still got thieves and wife beaters among us. Plus, some of the truckers can get a little violent after five or six drinks. Usually a night in the cells does the trick. They pay the fine and head off on their way."

"How far away is Proctor's Farm from here?"

"Few miles. The problem is it is down a dirt track off the main road. It's a rough road and you'll be isolated out there."

"I understand; but we need to see what is there. We have come this far."

"That you have. I tell you what. Young Deputy Cole over there will escort you to the farm. Hopefully his presence will deter any bandits from trying anything. They usually know better than to interfere with a lawman."

"Ah, jeez really, boss. It gives me the creeps out there," the deputy whined from the other side of the room.

"Do as you're told, son. Wouldn't kill you to do some work around here anyway!"

The deputy sunk back into his seat, defeated.

The sheriff turned his attention back to Harry and Victoria and said, "Sorry about him, my sister's boy. I promised I'd look after him before she passed. He's a good kid but lazy."

"I appreciate all the help we can get, sheriff," Harry said.

"Good, you had better stay in the motel down the road. Leave first thing tomorrow. Roads are treacherous after dark. Coyotes and other creatures rove in packs, and the raiders tend to be more active once the sun sets."

"Thanks. Where is the motel?"

"Back down the road about half a mile, you can't miss it."

"Alright."

"Meet back here at nine tomorrow. Cole over there will be ready and take you where you need to go. You hear that, boy! Nine A.M!"

"I heard you, boss!" young Deputy Cole said, not looking up from the magazine he had retrieved.

Harry and Victoria pulled up outside a shoddy-looking motel. It only had six rooms, all in a line. The metal sign was weathered and covered in black dust. Life seemed hard out here. The townsfolk may not have had the same troubles with pollution and air quality as the city folk had, but the threats of drought and famine were real and if the trucks stopped coming, then so would the supplies. Harry wondered if the years of war had done irreversible damage to the planet, and that they were all living on borrowed time, digging and growing what they could, just to eke out a few more years of existence. It was evening, and the setting sun made the sky above them glow in a burnt orange colour. A truck towing three paint-chipped cargo containers was parked; the driver must have fancied a night in a real bed and not in his cab for a change.

Harry suggested they get separate rooms to keep up appearances, which Victoria agreed with. The motel clerk was a frail old woman whose hands shook when she handed them their keys. Despite the hardships out here, life expectancy was probably a little higher than in the city. Having not seen skin so leathery and wrinkly in some time, Harry was amused by her slow, shaky movements.

He took the room next to Victoria and told her to knock if she needed anything. He didn't want to push it and suggest they share a room, despite how much he wanted to hold her again and to taste her lips. Distracting himself, he got to unpacking some equipment. He drew his revolver and fixed a small reflex sight to it. Knowing that if he had to fire from a moving vehicle, he would struggle to get a sight picture or take an accurate shot quickly, so any advantage would help. He wondered if he should have requested more firepower, perhaps a long-range rifle or an automatic submachine gun. Although, he wasn't the best shot with these kinds of weapons and rarely fired them, they were reserved mainly for the tactical teams. He checked the rest of his equipment over and ensured it was functioning correctly. The two heavy, silver-coloured flashlights both worked and were fitted with fresh batteries. His handcuffs were oiled and rust-free. He did wonder how they would fare if Harry found the killer out on the farm – he was out of his jurisdiction, not that anybody would care. He was more concerned about how he would transport them the hundreds of miles back to the city and if the car's trunk would be big enough. His gun belt and leather cuirass sat on a wooden chair in the corner of his motel room. He opened a packet of vacuum-packed protein nuggets and nibbled on them as he repacked his equipment.

As he closed his bag, he heard a knock on the door followed by Victoria saying, "Harry. Harry, come quick!"

He grabbed his revolver from the holster and bolted for the door. Ripping it open, he levelled the barrel of his gun to see Victoria with her back to him.

"What is it?" he said.

Victoria turned around and said, "Put that thing away and come out here."

Harry stuffed the gun into his rear waistband and stepped out onto the dirty parking lot. "What is it?" Harry asked.

"Look up."

Harry did what she said and was amazed when he saw hundreds of tiny glowing spots in the dark sky.

Keeping her head fixed on the beautiful sight above them, she said, "I can't remember the last I saw this many stars, Harry,"

"Me neither," Harry said, his eyes also transfixed on the miniscule white dots.

"There is very little light pollution out here," Victoria said. "Look, there!" She pointed at something which flashed for an instant and then disappeared.

"Must be a shooting star, you should make a wish."

"Look, another one. And another! Might be a meteor storm. Have you ever seen anything this amazing?"

"No. Never."

The show went on for a few minutes as dozens of stars shot across the darkness, each one grabbing the attention of them both, keeping them mesmerized and enchanted by their beauty and spectacle. The clouds eventually shifted and put an end to the nighttime entertainment.

"That was wonderful," Victoria said with pure glee, finally levelling her head and looking at Harry.

"It was indeed."

"I don't want to be alone tonight, Harry."

Neither did he, so neither of them spent the night alone.

CHAPTER FOURTEEN

The pair arrived at the sheriff's office just before nine that following morning. A sizeable 4x4 truck was parked outside the front. It looked like it had once been used by the military – beneath the tan paint job were spots of green which was likely its original colour. It had a boxy straight look, lacking any modern curves and had an open bay on the rear, where other deputies could stand. A row of spotlights were fixed to its roof, although one was cracked.

They stepped into the sheriff's office to see Deputy Cole strapping his gun belt to his waist. His six-shooter was longer and more intimidating than Harry's. He wore the same hat as his uncle, along with a bulky and uncomfortable looking ballistic vest which would probably do a better job at stopping a bullet than Harry's cuirass would. Harry hadn't shaved that morning, and Victoria was enjoying his rugged look.

"You ready to go?" Cole said.

"Ready when you are, Deputy," Victoria said.

The deputy blushed again and then looked away.

Sheriff Miles stepped out of a side room and said, "Young Cole here will escort you to the farm limits. He'll keep watch for you, but I'll need him back before sundown."

"We don't plan on being out there that long," Harry said. "At least we don't want to be."

"Alright, good luck out there. Be sure to share your findings, won't you. I wouldn't mind knowing myself what is out there."

"I will."

"Oh, take this. It's a handheld radio, Cole will have the other, you can communicate on the road." Sheriff Miles handed them a heavy brown brick with a long thin extendable antenna and a speaker.

The trio nodded at the sheriff before stepping outside.

"Alright, city slickers," Cole said. "Follow me on the highway for a few miles, we will then see an old sign for the farm. It's about two miles off the main road, over some hills in a valley. If it gets stormy out there, which it may, we will have to stop the cars and wait it out. It's too dangerous to drive through a dust storm, you can get turned around easily or drive headfirst into a ditch. We won't want to lose each other out there."

"We will follow your lead," Victoria said.

Cole tipped his hat, having finally found some confidence in front of the redhead and climbed into his big truck. It took several seconds of whining and spluttering before the engine finally came alive. Cole planted his foot a couple of times to get the fuel flowing. Despite their own car's impressive ride height, it paled in comparison to the towering truck in front of them. It lurched its way from the kerb before pulling away at quite a pace. Harry had little trouble keeping up with it though as they exited the small town. The inhabitants stepped out of the homes and shacks to admire the strange people one final time as they left.

Once they were clear of the town's limits, Harry hit the cruise control and kept a good distance from the deputy so he had time to react to anything.

"What do you think we will find out there?" Victoria said.

"No idea, hopefully some damn answers. We are still no closer to finding out who plugged, sorry, killed your father. We know it was one of these cultists, but we still don't know who."

"If you find the killer, then what? Is the case closed? Are you going to move onto the next one?"

"I doubt it, things are changing in the city. If we don't find out who is running the show and put an end to the madness, I am worried something else, something bigger, is going to happen."

"So am I. I have never been this worried about anything before."

"Neither have I, and I have worked plenty of dark and twisted cases in my time. But something about this one puts me on edge."

They followed the deputy for what felt like an eternity before he flicked on his left signal. Harry slowed and followed the truck as it turned off the endless highway onto a rough road. Even the large tyres and suspension would struggle to make this journey comfortable. The truck up ahead kicked up a lot of dust so Harry had to drop back even further and follow sheet of grey powder ahead of him. They drove in a straight line for a couple of minutes;

eventually the handheld radio crackled and Cole said, "You two doing ok back there, over?"

Victoria grabbed the heavy radio, pressed the talk switch, put on a funny accent said, "We sure are, cowboy. How you doing… over?"

The radio crackled again. "Good, Ma'am, sorry for the view back there, just follow my tracks and dust if you get lost."

"We will. Let me know when we are close."

But Cole didn't transmit again. The radio went quiet.

"Something wrong?" Harry said.

"I don't know," Victoria said.

The truck ahead came to a stop suddenly and Harry had to hit the brakes.

"What is it, Deputy!?" Victoria asked down the radio.

Crzzz…crzz… the radio crackled.

"You aren't coming through. What's wrong?"

The crackling stopped. Then Cole spoke: "Raiders! To our right!"

They turned to see a convoy of grisly-looking vehicles making their way across the grey desert landscape towards them. One truck, bigger than the other vehicles, was rusted, covered in spikes and led the pack. Two hoverbikes followed. They were nimble, powered by small thruster engines and didn't require wheels. They were used heavily during the war. The technology was volatile and was prone to failing or exploding if not well maintained. The riders were clad head to toe in black leather. They kept their thin bodies low against the bikes. Their feet rested against pedals, and they used their arms to steer. The bikes were just as rusted and battered as the truck, likely patched together from pieces of other vehicles. Many of the panels were missing, exposing an arrangement of wires and pipes. Another wagon, similar in size and shape to Cole's vehicle, took up the rear of the convoy.

"Do you want to turn back?" Victoria said.

"No." Crzzz… "They will probably expect that and have something planned. Keep pushing, if we can take one or two out, we may be able to scare the rest away."

"Alright, cowboy, we won't be able to see much behind you though."

"I'll go off road, my vehicle is bigger than yours, maybe I can ram them into some of these boulders you see out here."

The deputy turned off the road and gunned it towards the pack of metal hyenas heading straight for them.

"Can you drive this thing?" Harry said.

"Sure. Why?" Victoria said, looking beyond Harry at the convoy rapidly approaching them.

"Trust me, let's switch seats."

Harry dived onto the backseats as Victoria shuffled into the driver's seat. She hit the gas pedal as the wheels spun, struggling to find traction before the car shot forward.

"What are you doing back there, Harry?" Victoria said, peering over her shoulder and then at the two hoverbikes closing in on them. "Whatever you have planned, do it fast!"

Harry lifted a sheet of the lever action shotgun and opened the breech; he loaded as many shells into the magazine as would fit before cocking it. Victoria hit a pothole which sent a couple of shells flying out of his hand.

"Take it easy, dammit!" he shouted in frustration.

"You try driving on this road! Harry, to our right!"

Harry looked over to see a hoverbike closing in on them at a rapid pace. A strange fuzzy haze trailed them, along with a long string of black smoke. They made a loud, high-pitched squeal when they accelerated.

"Turn the car off the road onto the desert!" Harry commanded.

Victoria didn't argue, she just did what he said and drove towards the oncoming bikes. Harry lowered the rear window and leant out with the shotgun. He placed the wooden butt in his shoulder and took aim.

The hoverbikes continued to quickly close the distance.

"Keep it steady," he said, trying to not let the rough terrain affect his aim. When one of the hoverbikes was about ten meters away, he pulled the trigger and a cloud of smoke and pellet shot out the end of the barrel. The shotgun kicked back harshly into his shoulder. Harry flicked his right wrist, cocking the lever and ejecting the spent shell out of the top. The buckshot glanced off the hoverbike as the rider

made a hard left to avoid a follow-up shot. No real damage had been done, and Harry would have to wait for another pass. A thunderous explosion was heard ahead of them.

Crrrzzz… "Dynamite! They got sticks of dynamite I think!" Cole shouted down the radio.

The rest of the raiders were swarming the deputy, firing at him with pistols and rifles. One of the raiders stood on the cab of the wagon and lit a stick of explosives. He threw the stick towards Cole and narrowly missed him. The resulting explosion shook the ground and made a deafening crack as sand shot up in the shape of a mushroom.

"We gotta help him, Harry," Victoria said. She turned the wheel and was now driving straight towards the gaggle of metal and rubber.

"We do. But we got our own problems as well."

There was a hoverbike approaching either side of them now. One of them shot more black smoke out than the other. Perhaps Harry had done more damage than he expected.

"Victoria, you still got that gun to hand?!"

"Yeah!"

"Good, when that bike on your left closes in, I want you to point it at the rider and empty the magazine. Don't aim for the bike, it won't do any damage."

"I think it only has about seven shots!"

"That's plenty," Harry growled. He pulled a set of tinted goggles over his eyes, keeping the dust from affecting his aim. The hoverbikes let out an almighty squeal as they accelerated towards the car. Leaning of the rear door again, this time facing towards the back of the car he fired two shots at the raider. The rider made some evasive manoeuvres, avoiding the volleys of buckshot. Victoria checked her shoulder to see the raider closing in on her. She had to try and avoid sink holes and large rocks which littered the desert floor and swerved harshly. Up ahead was Cole, firing his heavy revolver out of his window at the raiders that circled him like scavenger birds above a carrion. He hit one who was standing on the back of the wagon and sent his limp body falling onto the hard dusty ground. But he was quickly replaced by another leather-clad figure from inside the wagon.

Victoria readied her pistol; she lowered her window and tightened her grip on the small handgun. Harry's rapid firing of the shotgun kept his raider at bay, but he quickly ran dry and needed to reload. Glancing over towards the left side of the car he saw the other raider closing in. He chucked the shotgun onto the seat and drew his revolver.

"Ready?!" He asked.

Steering the car with one hand, she confidently said, "Yeah, let's do this."

The hoverbike closed in on them like a shark, ready to ambush its prey. The leather-bound rider pulled a long-barrelled pistol out of a holster and pointed it at Victoria.

"Now!" Harry shouted and fired through the left passenger door window, shattering the glass. Victoria did the same; she squeezed the trigger repeatedly until the slide locked back. Harry lined the sight up with the rider's black body and fired until his revolver ran empty; the gun just made a clicking sound as the hammer struck the empty cases within the rotating drum. The rider slumped off the bike and sent it racing out of control until it hit a boulder and exploded into a ball of fire and metal.

"Nice!" Harry cheered.

Before they could think about celebrating, a burst of rounds smashed through the car. Harry ducked for cover and Victoria slouched further into her seat, barely able to see over the dashboard. She caught sight of the other raider firing at them and swerved to try and knock them off balance. The rider dropped back and let Victoria swipe wildly with the heavy car.

The raider took the opportunity to load a fresh clip into their gun. Harry reached for the shotgun which was still on the back seat and started stuffing more shells back into the magazine.

"Harry! I'm out and he's on our left again!" Victoria screamed, clocking the rider in her wing mirror. The rider got himself closer this time, wanting to get a clean shot on her. As they came level with the car, Harry pushed the rear door open. He lay on his back and tilted his head to get a view. Placing the barrel of the shotgun just past his face, he pulled the trigger. The blast from the barrel rattled his senses as the buckshot exited it. Working the lever, ejecting the spent case onto his body, he fired again and again. The hoverbike spurted and shot out hot oil and smoke. The rider struggled to maintain control of his vehicle, which eventually caught fire. The rear half exploded, splitting the bike in two and sending the rider through the air to their death.

"You got him!" Victoria shouted with joy. It was short lived though as another explosion followed by a fireball was seen ahead of them. "Oh god. Harry, no!"

Harry sat up straight and saw the poor deputy's truck on fire. There was no way he could have survived a blast like that, and he deserved better. So much for raiders leaving the law alone. Perhaps they were just as desperate as everyone else in this miserable world.

"Bastards," Harry said, loading another handful of shells into the shotgun.

"How many of those you got left?"

"Not many, I need to make these count."

"What do you need me to do?"

"Get me close, if I can take out the drivers, maybe we have a chance."

The truck and the wagon closed in on them. Victoria turned a sharp left and floored it. The V8 would probably be able to outrun them, but it would drink fuel, and the raiders knew these lands and would likely track them to their destination.

She pushed on through the desert, not knowing where the dirt track that led to the farm was now. They could worry about that later, first they had to deal with the violent scavengers hot on their tail. The wagon closed in on them; it was fast for its size, probably heavily modified with nitrous injection.

"Let the wagon get close to us. Then I will go for the driver," Harry said.

Victoria eased off the gas and allowed the wagon to creep within range of her gunner. He leant out of the window again and fired at the wagon's narrow windscreen. Buckshot smashed into the glass, creating two dozen small holes. It narrowly missed the driver, but Harry saw blood on the passenger side. He cocked the shotgun again, ready to take another shot. The driver accelerated and drifted to the right. Another raider appeared on the rear cab, lighting a stick of dynamite. He switched his aim to the exposed bandit and fired repeatedly, praying that at least one of his shots found its target. Once the gun smoke cleared, Harry couldn't see the raider anymore. He was almost blinded when the truck exploded into a thousand pieces. The car was peppered with shrapnel, and it was a miracle neither of them had caught any.

"Fuck, Harry!" Victoria screamed as she gunned it past the ball of fire.

One of Harry's goggle lenses had cracked, so he lifted them above his eyes. "Just the truck left now."

"What's the plan?"

"The same as before, let it close in and I will go for the driver again."

The truck caught up with them but adopted a different method of attack. Its passenger opened the door and leant out as far as his arm would allow. He fired rapidly at them with an old metal submachine gun. Harry fired back blindly as Victoria swerved the car, trying to avoid the hail of bullets raining down on them. The shotgun ran dry, and Harry hadn't reloaded his revolver. Victoria slowed the car and swerved into the truck, which ripped off one of the rear doors.

"Dammit!" she screamed.

Her hands gripped the wheel so tight her knuckles turned white as she desperately tried to get control of the car again. The truck swiped at the car, smashing into it. The raider was so focused on catching his prey he didn't notice the thick piece of rock ahead of them. By the time he saw it, it was too late. They pulled the steering wheel sharply to the left, causing the truck to flip onto its side and slide along the dirt until it eventually came to a stop. It left a trail of metal, oil and wood behind it. Victoria slowed the car to a crawl before stopping completely.

"I think that's the last of them," she said.

"I think...I think you're ri..."

Before Harry could finish his sentence, a body leant over the roof of the car and pulled him from his seat.

He tried to get to his feet, but he was met with a strong kick to the side of his face and fell backwards. The raider had jumped onto the car when the truck made a swipe at it. A familiar metallic taste of blood pressed against the tastebuds in his mouth as he scrambled backwards. His attacker stood atop the car sporting leather like the others and had a bandana wrapped around his face. Copper goggles with extended lenses obscured his eyes; metal bolts were fixed to the knuckles of his gloves. Victoria leapt out of the car, trying to find something to fend off their attacker. Harry's trembling hand reached for his revolver. He opened the drum and ejected the spent cases. All he needed was one clean shot and he could end the fight. Shakingly reaching for a cartridge with his left hand, he stuffed one into the drum. Before he could set it, the raider kicked the gun out of his hand and dropped his weight on top of him. He wrapped his hands around Harry's throat and squeezed. Victoria leapt on top of him, savagely clawing at his face, trying to get through the goggles and the bandana.

The raider shrugged her off and pushed her to the floor. Harry tried to get to his feet, needing to get some sort of advantage. The raider turned his attention back to him and swung his fist into Harry's ribs. His jacket and cuirass took most of the blow, but the sharp glove crashed against him which knocked the wind out of him. Harry's leather sap and flick knife were in his satchel in the back of the car. If he could get past the raider and grab it, he may have a chance. Victoria was dazed and on her knees. She had hit her head hard when she was pushed. The raider threw another punch, this time directed at Harry's head; ducking, he narrowly avoided the mighty blow. He tried to follow through with a punch of his own, but the raider stepped away and dragged Harry back towards the car before throwing him into it. Harry slumped against the exposed passenger doorframe as the raider stood above him. He grabbed Harry's jacket collar and raised his fist ready to finish the job. Harry closed his eyes and then heard a gunshot. The raider's grip loosened as he stumbled backwards. He turned and faced Victoria who held the revolver close to her body with two hands. Dabbing his wound gently before taking two steps forward, the violent forager of man and metal collapsed on the ground. He stopped moving entirely.

Harry grabbed hold of the car seat and lifted himself to his feet. Victoria came rushing to his aid.

"My God, Harry. Are you hurt?" she said.

"Yeah, all over," he groaned. "But I'll live. We gotta push on. We can't be far now."

"I don't even know where…wait…do you see that?"

"What?"

Victoria pointed at a wooden sign which read, PROCTOR'S FARM, NO TRESPASSING

"Nice, real nice."

Harry took several deep breaths before dusting himself off and spat a ball of blood and saliva onto the dirt beneath his feet. He patted the raider down, looking for anything of use. Inside his jacket was a wad of cash and some familiar flyers, all bearing the smokestack. The cult had been paying off the raiders. Or perhaps they had paid them to keep intruders at bay.

They inspected the damage to the car. The diesel cans were empty, having been riddled with bullet holes. They had been lucky enough not to have sustained a puncture. Harry reloaded his revolver and handed it along with his gun belt to Victoria. He loaded the last of the shells into the shotgun and cocked it. Once they had rested a short while, Harry started the V8 and pulled away from the trail of destruction behind them. The poor brave deputy entered his thoughts as they found their way back to the dirt road which led to the farm. Victoria was silent, although Harry could hear her sobbing quietly. Ahead of them were a small cluster of buildings, along with an old wooden barn. The roof of the farmhouse had collapsed; nobody lived there anymore. He crept the car forward and wondered what the hell there was to find out here.

CHAPTER FIFTEEN

The V8 groaned and spluttered to a halt just outside the dilapidated wooden barn. Harry popped the bonnet and was met by a cloud of white smoke. Pipes had been severed; fluid was leaking and the damage to the engine was catastrophic.

"Looks like we are walking home," Harry said, slamming the bonnet shut. He looked around the bleak farmyard at the damaged buildings and broken fences. What was once probably a vibrant place filled with living creatures was now nothing more than a depressing homage to a better time, a time full of hope and prospect. He retrieved his satchel and stuffed whatever he could carry into it.

The barn was large with a pointed roof. Its red paint was now dark and patchy. The silo adjacent to it had collapsed, its content had been scattered with the wind.

A metal weathervane stood on top of the old farmhouse, despite the majority of the roof now in ruin. It squeaked as it spun in the wind. Other than that, there were no other sounds. The place was deserted.

"There is nothing here, dammit," Harry said, frustrated.

"Let's take a proper look around," Victoria replied, trying to console him. She walked forward and tried to pull the barn doors open. They were stiff but budged slightly.

Pressing her hands against the wooden doors, she turned to him and said, "Help me with this, will you?"

Together they managed to drag the doors open. The inside of the barn was empty, save for some old tools in the corner. Rays of light crept through the gaps in the wooden beams. Harry stepped into the barn and retrieved a flashlight from his satchel and handed it to Victoria. He grabbed the other and flicked it on. He followed the beam of light across the barn walls until he was facing the wall opposite the open doors. It wasn't completely dark in the barn and Harry could see without the light, but he used it to focus his attention in the hope that something would stand out to him. Perhaps a clue as to why they were there or some sign of life. They stepped deeper into the barn. Harry held the shotgun by the fore-end with his right hand. Without a sling, he would have to carry it.

Victoria stepped ahead of him and heard a clunking noise beneath her feet. "You hear that?" she said.

"What?"

"Listen."

Victoria walked on the spot, slowly stamping her boots on the ground.

"Yeah," Harry said. "You're stood on something metal."

They dropped to their knees and brushed the dirt away to reveal a metal trap door. Victoria looked up at Harry and said, "We need to see what's down there."

Harry rubbed his jaw and then nodded. He found the handle, twisted it and opened the door. Beneath it was a rickety set of wooden stairs leading into a dark corridor.

"You first," Victoria said, clearly afraid of what lay ahead of them.

Harry slowly lowered himself down the old stairs which creaked beneath his feet. Once he stepped onto the concrete floor beneath him, he helped Victoria and then pointed the flashlight down the long path which ran past the edge of where the barn would be.

"This must run all the way past the farmhouse," Victoria said, also shining her flashlight into the void. Harry took a step forward and the black corridor illuminated itself. The lights fixed to the concrete walls came on automatically, lighting the path ahead of them.

They shared a worried glance and then pushed on. They walked for what felt like a mile until they came to a heavy metal door with a rotating dog handle like one would find on a submarine. Harry took hold of the round handle and rotated it until the door unlocked and jolted forward.

He stepped through, followed by Victoria, into a vast room stacked from ceiling to floor with what must have been several hundred cylindrical metal containers.

"What is all this?" Victoria asked. She walked towards one of the containers and held the torch up to the label.

Turning his torch back on, he did the same. He wiped his hand over the dusty white label and inspected the black lettering.

"Zeron gas…" he said.

Victoria turned to him and said, "Did you say zeron gas?"

"Yeah, that's what this one says."

Victoria inspected the containers in front of her and saw they all contained the same thing.

"What is this stuff?" Harry asked.

"Volster created it. I mean the company did. It's a toxic gas that is highly lethal. It was designed during the war but never used. The company created huge amounts of it and were ready to deploy it but were never given the go-ahead by the government. Once the war was over, they were tasked with disposing of it without the public finding out."

"I guess we found where they hid it. Why did they have to keep it a secret?"

"Because the government didn't want to be seen as desperate enough to use chemical weapons. And neither did Volster. It wanted to maintain the image that everything it produced was for the betterment of mankind. Although that ideal eventually faded. Now Volster will produce whatever is financially beneficial to them."

"Is this what Jasper wanted us to find?"

"I don't know. How does this help anything?"

"Sssh. You hear that?" Harry said. He stuck his index finger to his dry lips and looked towards the source of the strange sound.

"What?"

"Listen."

The pair fell silent. A faint noise could be heard coming from another room beyond them. It sounded like a woman singing. Neither Victoria nor Harry spoke as they crept towards its source. They exited the large room through another metal door into another long corridor like the one earlier.

"I guess we follow this to the sound," Victoria whispered.

They softly stepped down the concrete hall until they reached their destination and found the door to be unlocked. Harry took hold of the shotgun and stuffed the stock under his arm. He placed his finger on the trigger guard and used the barrel to poke the door open. Beyond it was a room illuminated by candlelight. A gramophone played a song written by Celia Grey, a popular musician whose voice was soothing and delightful and popular on many radio stations. Her melody did little to calm their shattered nerves. Bookcases, wooden side tables and other furniture reminiscent of what was popular back in the city were present. Sat atop one of the side tables was a collection of black and white photos. Somebody lived here. Victoria picked up one of the photos and examined it. It was a portrait of a beautiful woman, probably around the same age as her.

"Come closer," a deep voice growled.

Harry placed the shotgun into his shoulder and took aim at the source of the voice. It came from the other end of the room which was shrouded in darkness.

"Who goes there?" Harry said, keeping the shotgun level. Victoria stepped close behind him and placed her hand on the holstered revolver.

"Come closer," the voice repeated.

They obliged, still remaining cautious and crept slowly towards the sinister voice. After three steps, the other side of the room became illuminated by a scattering of hanging lightbulbs, and they were faced with a monstrous figure attached to the wall. A body was on a mount with its arms extended like it was being crucified. Long brass pipes and cables protruded from its back and fed into two huge mechanical pumps which raised and lowered alternatively. The body was pale, malnourished and could have easily been mistaken for a corpse. Its rib cage was visible, along with its hip bones. A small dirty cloth covered its genitals. Neither knew if it was a male or female.

"What the hell is that?" Victoria whimpered, frightened by the grotesque sight in front of her and tightened her grip on the holstered revolver.

The body slowly raised its head. An oxygen mask was fixed to its face. The tube ran down from the mask behind its torso and was lost in the network of pipes. The technology would make the proudest of Black Lungs wince. Harry had never seen anything like this before. He didn't really know what he was looking at. Was the figure alive? Were these machines keeping it that way?

The body opened its eyes. They were yellow, bloodshot and terrifying. Harry slowly lowered his shotgun, mesmerized by the sight in front of him.

"Welcome...Detective..." The body groaned, seemingly struggling to talk. Its words were slow and spaced apart. The voice was distorted by the uncomfortable-looking mask strapped to its face.

"How do you know me?" Harry asked.

"We... have been watching you for some time now..."

"Who's we?"

"My… children."

Out of the shadows, either side of the creature stepped two cultists. Harry raised his shotgun again and trained it on one of them. Victoria took a step forward, pressed her shoulder against his and drew the revolver from her holster.

"You are…quite…safe…"

"Uh huh," Victoria muttered. "Tell that to the one who tried to murder me…"

Harry kept his eyes on the cultists who stood staring at them. They stood like the others with their hands stuffed into their sleeves. Neither moved nor spoke, they just stood guard, staring.

"You…are quite…safe, Ms Volster…" The body coughed and wheezed. "Detective…you…have come here for answers, yes?"

"Yes."

Harry didn't let his eyes leave the cultist in front of him.

"Then…listen…Smoke City is an evil place…for too long…the city has allowed the evil to rise and stand tall in those…towers. The people who live…beneath you are dying and need to be saved…" The body coughed heavily again and spluttered, "Esmeralda…"

"Yes, Leader?" The female cultist in front of Harry answered.

"Continue…please…"

The body coughed loudly again and wheezed. The few sentences he had managed to say had taken their toll.

The cultist positioned herself in front of the crucified figure, cleared her throat and said, "Smoke City is a disease. Its people are oppressed and suffering unnecessarily so the rich can continue to live their perfect lifestyles in the safety of their concrete triumphs. We now have an opportunity to upset this balance of power and start anew."

"So what?" Harry said. "Your whole thing is just another eat the rich to feed the poor fiasco?"

"It is so much more than that, detective."

"Oh really? Because so far I am still investigating a murder of one of the city's wealthiest men, and now you say you want to flip the scales?"

"Detective. The city is dying. The air is so toxic that thousands of people die from it every year, no matter how many pills or medication they consume. Do you know why fuming is on the rise?"

"No."

"Because it is produced and distributed by Volster and its rivals. The drug labs you and your fellow officers raid are merely fronts and distractions. It is supplied by the very companies that sell treatment for it. There is nothing anyone can do about it. People have tried to reveal the truth. And they have all been silenced."

"Is this why you and your gang came to be?"

"We…we have all lost many family members in Smoke City. Whether it be through the toxic air, drugs or by the corrupt system that should protect them."

"I don't believe Volster created fuming. It became an issue after the war."

"It…" The Leader groaned. "It was created during the war…I was…one of the first test subjects…"

Esmeralda paced up and down and said, "It was introduced as a combat stimulant but didn't have the desired effects. It was too potent, causing vivid hallucinations that rendered most soldiers useless and addicted. The first batch had other long-lasting effects which ate away at the body causing respiratory problems. Most didn't survive. They began to work out the kinks, but it was still too addictive. Soldiers began to steal from one another and in some cases, kill each other for extra doses. Once the war was over, the company had a surplus of the drug. Instead of disposing of it, they began drip feeding it into the undercity, keeping a huge chunk of the population docile and dependent on it. The city would be distracted by it, ignoring the greater societal problems."

"So what's your end game? You going to keep bumping off rich men and their help?"

"Their help?"

"Yeah. Your gang murdered a lowly lift operator and stole his uniform."

"Do you mean Reggie?"

"Yeah…"

The cultist laughed and then looked to her left. Out of the shadows stepped a man with a freshly shaven head, smiling at them.

"Reggie!" Victoria screamed.

The cultist looked back at Harry and continued, "Reggie understood our plans and sees our vision."

"What is your vision?" Victoria said. "How do you plan on carrying out your revolution?"

"I will offer you a choice…detective…" The Leader groaned.

"Go on…" Harry said.

"We will explain our plan, and you can return to your superiors and warn them…or you can allow it to happen… and give the city a chance at a…. a better future."

Esmeralda took a step forward and said, "The gas you saw in the room behind you has been entering the city for weeks. We have been placing it at different locations and will release it when the time is right."

"It won't do you any good," Victoria said. "It's heavy, and will sink into the undercity. You will be harming the people you want to save."

"Sadly, we understand that we cannot save them all. Instead, we want to give the city a chance to save itself. That's why we have placed the gas down in the dark depths of the places you sky dwellers tend to avoid. The undercity's inhabitants will flee their homes and become refugees. The sky dwellers will have no choice but to take them in, bring them into their own homes and treat them as equals."

"You're all insane," Harry said. "Thousands of people will die!"

"A small price for a greater future," The Leader said.

Reggie smiled at Victoria and nodded at Harry.

"Why are you telling me this? Why not kill us now and carry out your plan?"

"Because, detective," Esmerelda said, "we want to prove to you that despite warning and despite evidence, the city will refuse to change or improve. The only answer is action. Action that will sadly be lethal."

The Leader took a deep breath and said, "Warn your beloved city mayor…warn your officials and watch them do nothing…You have three days."

"They will listen. I will stop this," Victoria said defiantly.

"If you choose not to warn them, we will give you what you want, detective," Esmeralda said.

"What do you mean?" Harry said.

"The location and identity of your wife's killer." Esmeralda produced a note from the sleeve of her robe and held it by her side.

"I don't believe you. He's dead."

"You never found him though, did you?"

"How do you know where he is?"

"He sought us out and confessed, he wanted to be born again in the smoke like we had."

"Tell me his name."

"We will give your everything you want once we enact our plan."

"Tell me, godammit!"

"You have been given a choice. Even if you tell your superiors, we doubt they will believe you. Why not let this happen, detective? Why not give the city the chance to change it so desperately needs?"

Harry raised the shotgun again and took a step towards Esmeralda. His eyes darted between the cultists and their deformed leader above them. Reggie and the remaining cultist closed in on the pair. Esmeralda held her gaze steadily on Harry, not deterred by the barrel pointing at her face.

He had to think of something and fast. Except he couldn't just murder the woman in front of him and take what he wanted, regardless of how badly he wanted answers to what had troubled him for years. He knew if he killed her, the other two cultists would be on him in a flash, and they would likely meet his end in this dark basement in front of this creature suspended in the air. He glanced at the body then made his move. Moving the barrel away from Esmeralda's head, he fired at the clutter of metal pipes. Steam shot out of the many tiny holes caused by the buckshot. The Leader groaned in agony. The cultists turned and assessed the damage. Harry fired again, this time at another cluster of pipes. More smoke and fluid escaped. The sound of the blasts in the room was deafening. Victoria leant forward and grabbed the note from Esmeralda's hand and pushed her against the piping. Harry grabbed Victoria by her wrist and pulled her away. The cultists turned to tend to their leader; one hurried to a control panel full of dials and switches and began tampering with it.

Victoria did her best to keep up with Harry as they made their way past the room full of the toxic gas and back into the long concrete hall, towards the stairs. Neither looked back; instead, they focused on reaching the trap door and getting back outside. Harry took the stairs two at a time. Victoria scrambled onto her hands and knees and dragged herself upwards, through the trap door and back into the barn. He lifted her to her feet and then started towards the barn doors. As they stepped through them, they were met by a man holding an engraved pistol. He was dressed in green and brown tactical gear. A bandana obscured the lower half of his face. He wasn't a cultist, nor was he a raider. Harry paused and waited a few moments to see what the man was going to do. He wouldn't be able to raise the shotgun fast enough if the man decided to point his pistol at them.

He was relieved when the man raised his free hand and lowered his bandana.

"Arthur?" Victoria said.

"You had both better come with me, quickly," Arthur said, holstering his pistol and turning away from them. He had parked his car next to the V8 which was now nothing more than scrap. Harry grabbed what he could from the trunk and chucked several bags to Victoria. They scurried towards Arthur's vehicle, which was a large six-wheeled pickup truck painted black with tinted windows. There were no markings or Volster company logos to be seen. He clearly did not want to advertise his presence out here.

Once they were aboard, Arthur started the engine and pulled away down the dirt track. Harry leant out of the window to see if anyone was following them, but he saw nothing.

Leaning forward from the rear seats, Victoria asked, "How did you know where we were?"

"The car has a tracker on it. Your brother was concerned about you and wanted me to keep an eye on you."

"Stalk me more like."

"What did you find down there?"

"I…I don't know. Those cultists, the ones responsible for my father's death, have terrible plans for the city. We need to get back quickly."

Victoria looked over at Harry, who was studying a piece of paper. He must have swiped the note from her when he pulled her out of the basement. She was angry at her brother for asking his aide to follow them, but also relieved that he had arrived when he had. No doubt they would argue the matter upon her return to the city. But right now she was glad to have someone as reliable as Arthur in her company. "What does it say?" she asked.

"It's an address, in the undercity."

"You aren't going to go there, are you?"

Harry said no more, he folded the paper and stuffed in into his jacket pocket. Arthur was silent as he drove along the dirt track, past the wreckages of the earlier battle.

"We will need to swing by the sheriff's office in Bonesville," Harry eventually said, producing a crumpled packet of cigarettes from his satchel. "I need to tell him what happened to his deputy."

"What are you doing?" Arthur asked. He glanced over at the detective as he stuffed a crooked cigarette into his mouth.

"What do you mean?"

"Don't smoke that in here."

Confused, Harry removed the cigarette from his mouth and assumed Arthur was used to being around cigarette smoke like everyone else was in the city.

"Here, take one of these."

Arthur opened the glove box and selected a small tin. Inside were the same cigarettes that Horus had given Harry during their first meeting. The man may have been an insufferable snob, but he had a good taste in tobacco. Harry selected two cigarettes and handed one to Victoria. Arthur grabbed a third and they all lit them using his metal flip lighter.

Harry inhaled the rich flavour and allowed it to sit in his lungs for a few seconds before exhaling slowly. He focused on the sound of the wheels driving over the dirt road and what his next move would be. He would have to try and call his office once he was back in Bonesville and warn Carter, although he suspected that without proof, they would dismiss anything he had to tell them. Taking another drag of the cigarette, he thought about what he had seen in that basement. How organised and dangerous The Children must be if their plans were real. He imagined the chaos that would engulf the city if it came to fruition. The police wouldn't be able to control the situation and there would be disorder and violence everywhere. Finally, he thought about what he would say to his superiors and what their reaction to the news would be. He mentally chastised himself for not ripping a label off one of the barrels. Now he would be going back empty handed, with just his word.

Arthur didn't ask them any more about their journey, nor about the wreckages behind them or the situation with the cult. He was stoic, reserved and focused. Harry was wary of him. Unsure whether to trust him or not, but right now, he too was grateful for his help as his plan didn't extend much past distracting the cultists and making a run for it. It had slipped his mind that their car was shot to pieces, and they would have had no way of escaping. They certainly wouldn't have been able to walk back to Bonesville, not without risking attacks from more raiders or wild animals.

"That was you, back in the foundry, wasn't it, Arthur?" Victoria said. "My brother had sent you to follow us."

"He had sent me to watch over you. And that's exactly what I was doing,"

"Either way," Harry said, "I am glad you turned up when you did. You got any more of those cigarettes left?"

CHAPTER SIXTEEN

SheriffMiles took the news of his deputy's passing about as well as any caring man could. Harry suspected it would hit him hard later that night, and he would drown his sorrows in a bottle like most lawmen. Frustratingly, the phone lines had gone down, so he was unable to put a call in to the precinct to warn them of the impending attack. He told SheriffMiles about what was out in Proctor's Farm and asked if he could set up a roadblock to inspect the cargo of any trucks that came through the town. He agreed, despite clearly becoming emotional as the news began to settle in. Apologising again, they hastily took their leave, not wanting to outstay their welcome.

Arthur remained in the truck and Harry told him to step on it as they left the small desolate town behind them. Arthur kept his foot planted firmly on the gas pedal as they traversed the empty highway. Rarely dropping below one hundred miles an hour. Harry inspected every truck they drove by, hoping to see the gas containers. So far, nothing. Perhaps the cultists were bluffing, and they hadn't shipped anything. He thought about what he'd been told about fuming. Whether Victoria knew about this or she was unaware of the dark secrets her company kept hidden. The trio snacked and smoked until they were close to the city limits. Arthur seldom spoke. Despite returning to the polluted metropolis, Harry was keen to put the dustbowl behind him and return to some familiarity. Arthur agreed to drop Harry off at the precinct. The attack was meant to happen in the next three days, which left little time to evacuate any citizens and search for the gas cannisters. Victoria followed Harry out of the car and told Arthur to keep the engine running. They stood on a busy platform surrounded by police officers coming and going from the entrance.

"Is it true?" Harry asked.

"Is what true?"

"About fuming? About Volster?"

"I don't know, I am going to find out myself now."

"Let me know what you find. I need to speak with my boss along with the commissioner."

"I will speak to Horus and even try to get an appointment with the mayor. You'll need help if an evacuation is needed, and a state of emergency is declared. I can pull some strings and call in some favours."

"I appreciate it. I had better get going."

"Ok."

Harry wanted to grab her and kiss her, but he felt the eyes of others on him, and on her. Instead, he patted her gently on the arm and then turned towards the entrance. Victoria smiled and then returned to the truck.

Before Harry entered the precinct, he stopped and stared at the road which ran through the building and the ones beyond. Was it worth saving? The city was his home, yet a part of him detested it; it had taken his beloved wife from him and ruined the lives of many more. But it was full of decent people, art, music, culture and other things that people had fought and died for. A change was needed, but people shouldn't have to perish for it. He considered his options: he could go to his home, above the fog; he could let the gas release and watch the chaos unfold; he could do his duty like a good cop and hope that the city made good choices, even if thousands of people had to die; or he could march upstairs and convince his superiors that an attack was imminent. With some luck, they would believe him and scour the undercity, alley by alley if they had to. They could find the gas, remove it and prevent anything from happening. He would give the feds the location of the farm, so they could apprehend The Leader and end this cult before it grew too great and too powerful. The city's status quo wouldn't change though. Even if he tried to expose the fuming scandal it would likely be quashed, along with his career. Then he thought about Caroline, what she would have wanted. His choice was made.

Harry caught a glimpse of himself in a mirror as he walked towards the detective's office. He was covered in black dust; his hair was a mess, and his appearance attracted disapproving looks from plain clothes officers and uniforms alike. Still, he couldn't care less, time was pressing. Chief Inspector Carter spotted Harry as soon as he walked into the office and gestured for him to come straight over.

"Damn, Harry," Carter said. "You look worse and worse every time I see you."

"David, I have some news."

"So do I. Jasper has confessed."

"What?"

"This morning, he confessed to his father's murder. He is going before a judge this afternoon."

"Who did he confess to?"

"You aren't going to like it."

"Who, Chief?"

"Beek."

"What? How? Why was Beek talking to him?"

"The commissioner was getting impatient while you were away, he sent Beek in. It was like Jasper took a liking to him and told him everything. Supposedly, his old man was going to stop sending him cash and cut him off, he confronted him about it and shot him."

"I'm not buying it."

"Look, neither am I…but we need to take the win on this one."

"What win, David?!"

"Keep your voice down, dammit. The whole office will be trying to listen in. What did you find on your little road trip?"

"Something big is going down. Involving something called zeron gas."

"Which is?"

"Something extremely dangerous. I found…I think I found the cult's leader; they told me that the cult have been importing this crap into the undercity and are planning on releasing it within the next couple of days."

"What does it do?"

"What do you think? Kill people."

"Why would the cult want to start harming the poor, I thought their whole shtick was hurting the rich?"

"They want to cause mass panic, force the city to accept the inhabitants from the undercity, tip the scales, make it so that they can no longer be ignored."

"It seems a little extreme, don't you think, Harry?"

"Yeah, but nothing has been normal lately. David, I don't think they are kidding. If we don't act on this, thousands of people may die, thousands more will be displaced. There will be mass panic, the city won't know what to do. We won't know what to do."

Carter turned away from Harry and placed his hands on his hips, he sighed and looked up at the ceiling. He eventually turned around and said, "Harry. I will pass on what you said to the commissioner. But I don't think he will buy it. We have rounded up a handful of these cultists and interrogated them. None of them have mentioned any attacks. They all just talk about smoke and cleansing the city."

"This is the cleansing. This is their plan. I am telling you."

Harry rubbed his clumpy, dry hair; flecks of black dust fell out of it and onto the green carpet.

"Go home," Carter said. "Take a shower and a couple days off. I will call you."

Angering now, but he knew if he pushed it anymore, he would risk a suspension or worse. His boss looked tired, likely fed up with the pressure from the brass and wanted this case closed quickly. Carter wouldn't push too hard against a full and frank confession and Harry didn't blame him.

"Before I go, can I talk with Jasper?" Harry asked.

"Why?"

"I just want to ask him a couple more questions, that's all."

"Fine, you can ask him in his cell though."

Harry exited the office and shut the door hard behind him, causing the shutters to flap against the glass door. He noticed the dismissive looks from the other detectives who sat at their desks, hiding behind a cloud of cigarette smoke. Once he was in the cell block, he checked his revolver into a lock box and made his way towards Jasper, who was sitting alone in a metal cage. The other cultists had been separated from each other.

Jasper's eyes lit up when he saw Harry open the cell door.

"Ah. Detective, good to see you again." Jasper hissed like a snake. All that he was missing was a forked tongue. "Tell me, was your trip beneficial?"

"I found your leader. He told me what your plan is."

"Yes."

"Is it true?"

"What do you believe?"

"Answer the question, Jasper."

Jasper leant back and placed his head against the concrete wall. He remained silent.

"You didn't kill your father, did you?"

Jasper continued to hold his tongue, he simply stared at the worn detective.

"Why would you confess to it? They will probably execute you."

"A small price to pay for a brighter future."

"What did your brother say to you? I saw him coming to the station to try and bail you out."

"He tried to convince me to rejoin him in the sky. I declined his offer, and the police also declined his bail money. My brother is beyond salvation."

"Do you know how many people will die if that gas gets out, is that a small price?"

"The city needs to be torn apart before it can be put back together. Yes, there will be casualties, but in time, the city will thank us."

"Where is the gas being stored? Where are they going to release it, and when?"

Becoming rageful now, the madman sitting in front of him knew far more than he was letting on.

"Oh, detective, even I don't know that. Tell me, have you gone to that address yet? The one scribbled on the note in your pocket."

"No. What's it to you?"

"I'd hurry; time is ticking. You wouldn't want to miss your opportunity now, would you?"

Harry lost it. He stepped forward and threw Jasper to the floor. Dragging him back up by his robe, he struck him once in the face.

"Where is the gas?!" Harry shouted, striking Jasper again. The sound of keys jangling got louder as the cell guard sprinted towards the commotion.

Jasper smiled, blood covered his gums and stumpy teeth.

It was through these bloody gums that he said, "Such fire, you should join us!"

Harry raised his fist again but held off on throwing another punch. The guard fumbled with the keys, desperate to unlock the door. He rushed into the cell and dragged Harry backwards.

"That's enough, detective!" the guard said.

Harry shrugged himself free and stomped out of the cell as the guard tended to Jasper's wounds. He retrieved his gun from the safe and made his way to the main elevator which led to the undercity. If he was quick, he could be down there before his boss found out about what had just happened in the cell. He had never struck a suspect before, no matter how much they infuriated him. He worried it could cost him his job, but he had to quash those concerns and stay focused. The last few days had been rough, and Harry was feeling their effects. He retrieved the folded piece of paper from his pocket and stared at the address. He needed to know if it was true, if Caroline's murderer was indeed still alive.

CHAPTER SEVENTEEN

A s Harry approached the large elevator, he spotted
Sergeant Murillo talking to two officers.

"Excuse me, sergeant," he said.

Murillo turned his attention to the detective and said,
"Jeez, you look a little worse for wear."

"Uh huh, look, sergeant, I need a favour."

"Shoot."

"I don't think Jasper killed his old man, and I know
he didn't kill your man. I think there is something more
going on here."

"You don't say."

"I need your boys to keep their eyes peeled for something."

"Go on."

"I think the cult have been smuggling barrels of toxic
gas into the undercity. There are these black cylindrical
containers with white labels on. It's zeron gas, supposedly
highly toxic."

"Where do you think we'd find them?"

"I don't know, on street corners, maybe inside parked
trucks or hidden somewhere. I think they are going to
release them in the next couple days. If they do, a lot of
people will die."

"Sounds a little wacko to me, detective."

"It is, but so are bald, robe-wearing zealots."

"You got a point, all right. I will brief my boys. Zeron gas you say?"

"Yeah."

"Never heard of it myself."

"Me neither, but I'm sure on this one."

"Alright, I'll trust you, detective, and I'll tell my boys to do the same."

"Thank you. I mean it, sarge."

Murillo nodded at Harry and then went back to talking to the other officers who had listened to the conversation with interest. Harry stepped into the elevator along with a handful of uniforms who climbed into an armoured support truck, ready for their shift.

***

"I am not buying all of this," Horus said. He stood staring out of the tall window in his office like an old emperor would when they wanted to admire everything they had conquered. Victoria had spent the last hour explaining what they had found beyond the city, and the threat they now faced. She had told him about the gas, how Volster had caused the fuming epidemic and what they must do to prepare themselves if the attack took place.

"Brother, listen. We need to trust Harry on this and pour resources into assisting with an evacuation. Or, at least, prepare emergency provisions to feed these people if they have to flee their homes."

"I cannot see how the authorities nor the police have allowed shipment after shipment of this gas to be smuggled into the city. It is simply preposterous." Horus reached for his cigarette holder and placed it in his mouth.

"You know how stretched the police are in this city, and you know damn well they focus their priorities on the ongoings up here rather than those that truly need it."

"You have always cared more about them then you have your own, my darling sister." Horus lit a match and placed the flame against the cigarette protruding from the thin black holder. He took a long drag then made smoke rings as he exhaled.

"They are my people, dear brother. I was born there."

"Indeed you were," Horus snapped, "but our father rescued you from a bitter and miserable future and gave you an opportunity to do so much better."

"He did, and I never saw my brother again. My real brother."

"Father did what he could to find him, to bring him up here with you. Sadly, he snuck out from the orphanage one night and was never seen again. But you know all this."

"He could have adopted him at the same time and not just used me as a PR stunt. It was conveniently kept quiet that I had a brother, even the press didn't report on it."

Victoria paced around the lavish room. Two expensive leather sofas stood in the centre of the room facing each other, separated by a lengthy glass coffee table. An expensive chandelier hung from the high ceiling.

"It was truly sad, why don't you ask your detective friend to look into it? See what he can dig up."

"Stop playing games, Horus. Are you going to help me or not?"

Horus took a seat on the sofa and leant backwards, crossing his legs.

"Perhaps this city could do with a tragedy, a real one. After all, the mayor is up for re-election soon."

"You can't be serious, dammit. Thousands of people could die."

Horus opened his hands, signalling to his sister that he was indifferent on the matter.

"You really are a bastard, you know. And I don't believe for one minute that Jasper killed Lucius."

"Of course he did, Father threatened to cut him off, and he didn't take it lightly."

"And you are just going to let him die?"

"Our brother made his choice when he started smoking that awful stuff. But let us be honest, he was lost years before then."

"He became addicted to chemicals our company designed."

"I have found no evidence of this, and since becoming acting CEO I have been privy to a lot of ongoings in the company."

"I doubt it is common knowledge, Horus."

Victoria continued to pace around the room, Horus finished his cigarette and downed what was left in his whisky glass. He stood up and staggered towards his sister.

"My darling Victoria, how I have always admired your spirit, your will to do the right thing."

He began to creep into Victoria's personal space, which made her feel uncomfortable. She could smell the liquor on his breath. Victoria took a small step backwards as Horus stepped forward. He raised his left hand and stroked her hair which she still hadn't washed since returning to the city. An icy chill ran down her spine. Horus grabbed a handful and yanked her towards him. She tried to push him away, but her brother was stronger than her and stood his ground.

"Get off me, brother. You are hurting me," Victoria said through gritted teeth.

"Does the detective hold you like this when he makes love to you?" Horus raised his other hand and tried to stroke Victoria's face.

She slapped him away and tried to wiggle free of his grasp. Horus raised his hand again, as if to strike her.

A throat was cleared from the other side of the room. They both looked over to see Arthur stood, watching them.

"You are late for your meeting, sir," he said.

Horus released his sister and brushed himself down. She took three long steps backwards before turning her back on him and walked away. She looked over at Arthur who gave her the slightest of nods. She did the same and continued to ignore Horus as he gathered his things and left the room.

***

Harry took a tuk-tuk cab to a small apartment building that stood by the foundations of The Hatcher Building, one of the city's original towers built by one of the first mega corporations. The apartment building was only fifteen storeys high and was dwarfed by the seemingly never-ending concrete monolith which stood above it. Homeless men and women loitered by the steps and shook their collection pots as Harry stepped past them. The communal door to the building was unlocked. Once Harry was inside, he climbed the creaky stairs until he arrived at the eleventh floor. He checked the number scribbled on the piece of paper and walked down the hall until he found himself stood on the other side of a door. Its green paint was peeling from the wood and one of the brass numbers hung upside down.

He wasn't thinking straight, and he knew this. His next few decisions would change his life forever, for better or worse. He thought about Caroline, how kind and caring she was, and how she would wholeheartedly disapprove of his current course of action.

Knocking on the door, Harry waited a couple of seconds then took a step back. The door opened but was held by a chain. A short man stood in the gap. The familiar scars on his lips were visible from years of fume abuse.

"Cornelius Foust?" Harry said.

"Yes?" the man behind the door answered sheepishly.

Harry had envisioned this encounter for years. He thought he had come to terms with Caroline's death but only felt anger and bitter resentment towards his inability to catch her killer. What kind of a detective couldn't solve the murder of his own wife? He wondered if he would regret this decision. Kicking the door as hard as he could, the chain snapped as the door flew open. Cornelius was a small, thin man, wearing a cotton jumper riddled with holes and a pair of dirty grey trousers. Ugly, with little hair, he backed away with a terrifying look on his face. Harry slammed the door shut behind him and pushed him onto a stained couch as he drew his revolver.

Cornelius placed his hands across his face and said, "Please, don't kill me, take whatever you want. I have no money!"

"Shut up!" Harry commanded.

Cornelius whimpered and lowered his head. Several cult flyers lying out on a side table drew Harry's attention away from the whimpering man.

"Three years ago, a clinic. You went in there and robbed it. Not before murdering the nurse there."

"Oh god, what? Three years ago…I was…I was on the fumes. I didn't know which way was up. I…I…"

"Tell me, dammit, do you remember her name?!"

"I…I…"

The clicking of metal as Harry pulled the hammer back turned Cornelius into a whimpering wreck.

"It was…Nurse…Quint…or Quinn or something."

Harry leant forward and grabbed the fearful mess by his jumper and dragged him off the couch and onto the hard floorboards. He knelt on top of him and placed his gun against his left cheek.

"She was my wife, you son of a bitch!"

"P…please…please…don't. I… I… have a family."

"Bullshit."

"I do! I do, I promise you!"

Where are they?"

"My…wife is at work, she works at the market…our daughter is with her, she is only a baby. Please, detective… don't…kill me."

"How do you know I am a detective?"

"They…they told me you would come and ask questions. They told me to let you in and tell you what you wanted to know."

"Who, The Children?"

"Yes…I…sought them out. I wanted to know if they could help my child. She is ill, you see, and the nurses at the clinics don't have the equipment to treat her and I can't afford a specialist. They promised us help and medicine, if I did certain things for them."

"What things?"

"If I tell you…will you let me live?"

"Tell me!"

Harry's hands were shaking he was so angry. But he took a breath and slowly pulled the barrel of his gun away from the terrified man's face. Taking a long step backwards, he lowered it. Cornelius lifted himself up and pushed himself away until his back was against the wall.

"They…" Cornelius whimpered. "They had me hide these drums all over the city. Me and a few others were given locations on a map. They didn't tell me what they were for."

"Did the drums have labels on them?"

"Most were blank, they had been ripped off. Although one of them was only partially removed. I could see it was a gas of some kind."

"I need you to tell me where you planted them."

"I…I can't."

"Why not?"

"If I do, they said they wouldn't treat my daughter."

Harry thought about threatening the crying man again, about sticking the gun down his throat and demanding answers. Then he saw how desperate he was. He looked at the wallpaper peeling off the walls and at the old broken children's toys stuffed in the corner. There weren't many fumers who kicked the habit, those that did rarely went on to do good things.

"Cornelius, they won't help your daughter. You need to go to your wife and get out of the city, find a way above the fog if you can, or leave entirely."

"Why?"

"Those drums you and the others have been handling. I think they are going to use them to kill thousands of people. They want to destabilize the city and cause a panic."

"God no, they said it was to improve the air quality down here. So my daughter wouldn't be sick anymore."

"They are lying to you. Have you got a map laying around?"

"Yea…Yeah, somewhere. You mind if I get up?"

Harry de-cocked his revolver and nodded. Cornelius stood up and groaned as he straightened his knees. He limped over to a side table and opened a drawer.

"Here, we go," he said, handing the sheet to Harry, "these were my allocated drop sites."

Harry inspected the document. The sites were spread out far and wide. There didn't seem to be any pattern or connection.

"Was it just you involved in this?"

"No."

"How many more?"

"People? Dozens of us, all with different locations."

God, if there were a dozen more of these maps floating about, with just as many sites, the damage would be apocalyptic.

"How are they hidden? Are they locked away somewhere?"

"I was told to leave some in alleyways, by the dumpsters. Others I left in the food stalls and compensated the owners. Some I even left in the truck and was told to walk home."

"Cornelius, find your daughter and wife and leave this place right now. If you don't, you'll all die."

"Does this mean you are letting me go?"

Cornelius stood with tears in his eyes, he was still shaking and at the total mercy of the man stood in his living room. He looked at the worn and tired detective and began to remember the day he'd stumbled back into that clinic. Despite being incredibly high, he recalled the pretty, kind nurse and how she tried to get him to leave peacefully again. He remembered a struggle, but not the finer details. Perhaps his mind had blanked it out, as he was so ashamed of what he had done. Either way, he knew the man would probably be justified in his retribution.

Harry couldn't answer, he just stared into the eyes of the frightened man who stepped backwards and began to rip open drawers and cupboards. Harry had killed, but he wasn't a murderer. Caroline entered his mind again, and he remembered how she always used to encourage him to do the right thing, even when nobody was looking. To show compassion and empathy and to strive to be a better man.

Eventually, Harry sighed and said, "I will let you live if you go find your wife and child right now and get the hell out of this town. If…If I ever see you again, I won't hesitate to shoot you where you stand."

"I…I promise, I will pack a bag and leave right away. God I am sorry for what I did to you. Truly, I am. If I could turn back the clocks I would."

"Good, tell me, before you go, how did you kick the habit?"

"What?"

"Fuming, not many people do."

"I…I met a good woman."

Cornelius went back to gathering his belongings and started to pack some bags with tattered clothes. He didn't notice the detective slip out of his apartment. Harry had to find a radio and fast.

CHAPTER EIGHTEEN

The saying was true: there was never a cop around when you needed one. Harry flagged down a tuk-tuk and told him to head to a nearby bazaar where he knew the support units would likely be patrolling. It wasn't long until he found their armoured truck parked against the pavement. Two shotgun-wielding officers stood guarding it, watching the market goers, exhilarated at the thought of catching one of these unhinged cultists .

Harry threw a wad of notes at the driver, not bothering to count it, and stepped out of the taxi.

Flashing his badge at the officers he said, "Detective Quinn, Homicide Division. I need to use your radio."

The support officer looked through his metal mask at the badge and then nodded; he slammed his heavy fist against the truck door, and it opened. Harry climbed a metal step and gestured for the driver to hand over the radio telephone. He requested dispatch to get hold of Sergeant Murillo and tell him to head to the corner of Bower Street and Fifth Avenue and look for anything suspicious. Harry kept the phone pressed to his ear as he dragged his finger across the map. He rattled off a list of locations and asked that units attend and look for any metal drums which had been recently placed there and anything out of the ordinary. The dispatcher was unhelpful, claiming that she had limited resources available and wanted to know more details before assigning officers without good reason. Harry nearly lost his cool with the old bat on the other end of the radio but insisted that this was an emergency and that lives were at stake. Once he had given out the final location, he gave his badge number and told the operator to shove her stinking attitude up her ass. The truck's driver chuckled beneath his mask as he took the phone from the frustrated detective.

As he climbed out of the truck, one of the armoured officers closed in on him and said, "Detective, that call sounded serious. What is going on?"

"I think…Jeez, I think domestic terrorism. As ridiculous as it sounds," Harry said. He lit a cigarette and looked at the buildings which surrounded him. Having not smoked nearly enough in the last few days, he was suffering withdrawals, mainly headaches.

"Ridiculous? Detective, this whole damn city is ridiculous. Look, I am the commander of this truck, and this zone is my responsibility. What do you need?"

"If you hear explosions, see anything strange like people panicking or crowds rushing, direct them to the nearest elevator and get them off the streets. If they are full, get people to high ground, spread the word. It'll mean more from you than me."

"Are the brass aware of this?"

"They are…"

"And let me guess, they don't give a damn?"

"What do you think?"

"I know they don't."

Harry thanked the officer before turning to walk in the opposite direction. It reassured him that there were still good men and women ready to fight for this city, even if it didn't always deserve them. It was a fifteen-minute walk back to the precinct elevator; he took the time to plan his next move if no attack happened. He would have to request that the feds head to Proctor's Farm to see if they would arrest The Leader, however that would look. But first, he would need to touch base with Victoria and see what she had come up with, hopefully she had some answers.

Harry made his way to the wide elevator doors which were open, officers were standing guard, ensuring nobody snuck on without a permit.

A young officer came jogging towards him. "Detective Quinn?!" he yelled.

"Yeah?" Harry said.

"I have Murillo on the radio, said he needed to talk to you right away."

"Hand it over."

Harry followed the officer towards his car who handed him the phone.

"Detective, it's Murillo. Dispatch got hold of me and told me to head to Fifth."

"You find something?"

"Yeah, detective. Look, I think you are on to something. One of my boys got hold of me and said he is looking at a small truck parked where you said it would be. I've come down to see myself. It's unattended, and one of the bums said it's been parked like it for days."

"Uh huh."

"The" ...crrzz.... "sheet" ...crrz...crzzz... "gas."

The radio crackled until it was nothing but white noise.

"Sergeant? Sergeant?"

"Sorry about that, detective," the officer said. "We have been having issues all day with the radio."

Harry hadn't heard a word said since the radio had died. Instead, he stood and stared at the cultist standing in the alleyway opposite him. It was Esmarelda, from the farm. She took a step backwards and disappeared into a sheet of gutter smoke like some kind of phantom.

"You ok, Detective?"

Not looking back at the young officer, he kept his gaze fixed on the alley and said, "If you get back in touch with Murillo, tell him to start getting people to the nearest elevator. I need you and the others to do the same."

"I can't let people up without the right permit, you know this, Detective."

"If you don't, people will die."

"What?"

Harry didn't explain any further. Instead, he walked across the street into the wall of smoke and drew his revolver. The alley turned sharply to the right where it sat between two brick buildings. As Harry stepped around the corner, Esmeralda was waiting for him.

"Good to see you again, Detective," she said.

"Skip the games. What do you want?"

"To inform you that due to your irresponsible actions, we have decided to implement our plan earlier."

"What do you mean?"

"We offered you a fair opportunity, Harry, and you decided to be selfish and betray our trust. Now you and this city will pay the consequences."

"What?"

"Listen." Esmeralda raised her finger towards her ear and smiled. As she held it up, the ground shook, followed by a loud crack, like thunder. Another crack, this time not as powerful, followed by another. A faint sound of screaming could be heard.

"What...What have you done?!" Harry screamed.

"I suggest you hurry to one of your precious elevators before it is too late."

Esmeralda didn't flinch nor attempt to flee, she stood firm like a statue found on the tops of many of the towers, judging the detective.

Harry raised his revolver towards her. Another explosion, this one closer. The sound of screaming and shouting became louder and more intense. Esmeralda didn't even blink. His hand trembled until his arm gave way and the gun sank until it was pointing at the ground.

"Tick tock, Detective."

Turning quickly, he started back towards the street. A crowd had formed and were pushing their way towards the police elevator. A line of cops, some wearing padded riot gear, carrying long heavy shields, stood firm. They had trained for times like this and were ready, except now wasn't an insurrection or riot, it was a panic, driven by fear and the sheer will to survive. The shouting and screaming from the crowd was deafening. Harry tried desperately to wade his way through the sea of people, to get to the officers and tell them to stand down. He fought his way through, elbowing and pushing those he could. A young girl fell to her knees and began to cry as she was separated from her mother. Harry pulled her to her feet as he pushed onwards through the rabble. She followed him until she found her mother again.

"Let them through!" Harry shouted, but it was lost in a sea of screams and shouts.

"Let them through, dammit, otherwise we are all going to die!"

The supervising officer stood firm, behind the line of officers who continued to shove the crowd and strike them with heavy wooden batons. Some were fixed with stun caps, which would leave the recipient with a nasty shock. One of the officers drove the tip straight into the chest of a panicking man and sent him onto his backside.

Screw it, Harry thought. He drew his revolver and fired a shot into the air, hoping that would be heard over the crowd. It did the trick as the crowd ducked and looked for the source of the shot. Many of the officers went to draw their firearms until a younger one recognised the detective and told them to stand firm.

"Officers, I am Detective Inspector Harry Quinn! I am the senior officer right now and I am ordering you to let as many people onto the elevator as you can. If you don't, them, me and all of you are going to die down here!"

The ground commander froze, unsure what to do. The young officer who Harry had spoken to earlier turned to him and said, "We had better help these people, damn the permits."

The commander was still doubtful and didn't speak, the crowd were beginning to get animated again. He could see how serious the detective was and went with his gut.

"Alright!" he shouted. "Let as many in as we can. Withdraw!"

The officers backed away from the crowd, keeping their shields facing towards them as they retreated into the elevator. The crowd followed, pushing forward, tripping over each other, wanting to escape the mayhem unfolding around them. Harry didn't know how fast the gas would travel nor where the nearest explosion had been. All he could do was follow the crowd and pray the elevator could handle the extra weight. He felt familiar metal beneath his feet as he stumbled onto the lift. There must have been several hundred people crammed into it, with more on their way.

"We need to shut the doors!" an officer bellowed. "We can't handle any more weight!"

The lift operator ripped the handle back and the doors began to come together. More and more people scrambled to get inside, some crawled on their knees, narrowly avoiding being locked outside or cut in two. Others weren't so lucky. The crowd screamed and cried when they saw a handful of frightened people split in half at the waist by the heavy doors as they slammed shut.

The elevator began to rise, and Harry heard the screams all the way to the top.

CHAPTER NINETEEN

E very police blimp the city had at its disposal were out patrolling the night sky. Their powerful spotlights scanned the concrete jungle beneath them. The military were being mobilized and due to arrive sometime within the next seventy-two hours. A state of emergency had been declared and the undercity's residents who had been lucky enough to escape were being housed in makeshift camps in various plazas dotted around the city. The plazas were huge platforms which connected buildings and were typically used as social hubs for the tower's residents. Many of them contained art galleries, museums and theatres. Now, great tents were being erected, full of uncomfortable wartime bunk beds to house the fearful refugees.

Harry stood on his balcony, watching the blimp's spotlights scan the cityscape. He took a sip from his whisky glass and ran his hand through his hair. He had managed to shower before the water ration was decreased again. He wondered what the likes of Horus Volster and the city officials were discussing right now, were they panicking or chastising themselves for not believing him and Victoria? Or were they working out how to spin this dire situation to their advantage? A feeling of guilt washed over him, but he reminded himself that he hadn't been the one plotting the destruction of a city for weeks. Despite his failed efforts, he had tried to save as many people as he could. When he'd arrived back at the precinct, he had slipped away during the chaos of the new arrivals and convinced a patrol cop to drop him off home. The phone hadn't rung yet. Chief Carter was probably far too busy to concern himself with the likes of one rogue detective's whereabouts. The news anchor on his TV set reported that the death toll was still unclear, but that it was expected to be in the thousands and that hundreds of police officers were still unaccounted for. The city's mayor was due to attend a press conference later that evening to announce the new emergency measures the city had planned. The anchor stated that The Children of the Smoke had revealed themselves to the public and had taken credit for the attack, citing that it would bring about great change for the city which would be appreciated by future historians.

The whisky had gone down too easily, so Harry stepped back into his kitchen and emptied the last of the bottle into the glass. As he stuffed another cigarette into his mouth, there was a knock at the door. He held the unlit cigarette between his lips and grabbed his revolver off the kitchen counter. Peering through the spyhole, he saw Victoria stood on the other side. She stepped inside and he quickly pulled her towards him, checking there wasn't anyone loitering in the hall. Hugging and kissing again. Harry spat the unlit cigarette onto the floor and pressed his lips against hers. She had also showered and changed, and Harry lost himself in her delicate touch.

In between kissing him, she said, "I'm so glad you are ok,"

"I almost wasn't," he said, pausing for a moment.

They didn't speak again until they had given themselves entirely to each other. As they lay naked in his bed, holding each other, Victoria rubbed her hand lightly against Harry's chest.

"What are you going to do now?" she asked.

"Wait until the phone rings and see what my boss wants from me. I can't imagine for a minute that he will want me to carry on with the case. Besides, your brother is taking the fall for your father's murder."

"He is, even though we both know he didn't do it."

"They'll make an example out of him." Harry lifted his free arm and draped it over his forehead. "They'll publicly execute him as a warning to the rest of the cult and anyone who is thinking about joining. Although I doubt many will now. Not immediately. The case will be closed."

"We can't just wait until they make their next move though. We need to find out what it is and stop them."

"Do we?"

"What do you mean?"

"We found out and we both tried to stop it and look where that got us. What is the point?"

"Don't talk like that, Harry. You are a better man than that."

"Am I?"

"Yes… I am afraid to ask but…"

"I found him."

"Did you kill him?"

Harry sighed and rubbed his eyes. "No, I wanted to, my God I wanted to. I had the barrel of my gun placed against his neck and I could have pulled the trigger."

"Why didn't you?"

"He wasn't what I had imagined. He was off the fumes, had a family and was trying to lead a normal life. I couldn't bring myself to do it. Caroline wouldn't have wanted it."

"I am glad. I couldn't imagine what you felt meeting him face to face."

Harry continued to stare at the ceiling. He reached over and grabbed two cigarettes from a packet and handed one to Victoria. Harry struck the match and lit them both. As he waved the match to kill the flame, his picture phone started ringing. Victoria looked at him but didn't say anything.

He remained still, hoping that the ringing would soon cease. It didn't, so he ripped the sheet off his naked body and stormed into his living room.

Pressing the cold horn against his ear, he flicked the switch. The image was fuzzy despite the adjustments he made, something was interfering with it, perhaps all the blimps floating around.

"Quinn," Harry said, still adjusting the dial to try and get a better picture.

"Harry," the voice said, "it's Carter."

Playing with the settings just enough, his worn and dishevelled looking boss appeared on the screen. His tie hung away from his neck and most of his shirt buttons were undone. A bead of sweat ran down his forehead.

"Chief."

"Harry, I need you down at the station, the commissioner is putting all cops on twelve-hour shifts until the army get here. He is putting a special task force together."

"It's a little late for that, don't you think?"

"Now isn't the time for that, I need you here."

"I didn't know you wanted me so bad. I'm flattered."

"Cut the bullshit. I know you have been through a lot, hell, one of the uniforms said you were down there when the bombs went off."

"All right, give me a couple hours and I'll be there."

"Now, Harry!"

"I've been drinking, David; you don't want me driving over there still buzzed, do you?"

"Fine, put a pot of coffee on and take a cold shower."

"I can't, they are rationing the water if you haven't noticed."

"Just get down here!"

Carter slammed the cone onto the receiver and ended the call. Harry stood staring at the blank screen, smirking, he had all but stopped caring about the case, the commissioner and what was expected of him. In his peripherals, Victoria appeared. She was naked save for the bedsheet she pressed against her breasts.

"You need to go, Harry. The city needs you."

"God, Victoria, you make me out to be something out of a kid's comic book. I am no saviour. I'm…I'm just a cop, and not even a particularly good one."

"Really? How many more people would have died if you hadn't gotten them onto that lift. They'll listen to you now, they have to."

"What are you going to do?"

"I am going to convince my deviant of a brother to supply more aid. People escaped with nothing more than the clothes they were wearing."

"That's good. People will need all the help they can get right now."

Harry dressed himself back into his detective garb and downed a chilled bottle of water that had been in the fridge for some time. He slowly began to sober. As he went to grab a dark brown hat off the rack, Victoria said, "A traditional tie and hat, even in these trying times."

Harry perched the hat on his head and said, "I think I need a bit of normality in these abnormal times."

"Don't we all, be careful out there. Keep me updated if you find anything."

"I will."

He left her a spare key and told her to take whatever she needed, not that he had much to take. The drive over was quiet. It was late, and most of the city's residents had locked themselves away in the relative safety of their beloved towers. Select inhabitants didn't want to lay eyes on the makeshift refugee camps that now cluttered their favourite social areas. Harry cruised a highway which ran adjacent to the wall of a wide building nicknamed 'The Arrow', given how its long opposing walls eventually met one another and formed a tip. A police blimp slowly emerged from below the highway, its spotlight shone over the road ahead of him. He likened it to a dragon from a children's fairytale, out hunting its prey. The fins were its wings, and the spotlights its fire. Another blimp navigated between a pair of towers ahead of him. He had never seen so many out at once. The city still tried to cling to a sense of normality, jazz music continued to play on many of the radio networks, and Harry even spotted what looked like a high society party through a tall window as he pulled off the highway. Men and women wore their best party outfits and ate exquisite-looking food. He caught a glance of what looked like a large bird, lying dead on the table. The partygoers seemed totally unconcerned with the troubles affecting the rest of the city, or at least pretended it wasn't happening.

The precinct's car port was rammed, which wasn't surprising if every cop had been put on twelve-hour shifts, the uniforms were probably now acting more like prison guards at the refugee centres, ready to quash anyone who protested against their new putrid living conditions amongst a sea of lavish apartments with empty bedrooms.

Once Harry had parked the car, he squirted a shot of mouth spray to try and hide the scent of any booze that may still be lingering, not that anybody would give a shit given the current circumstances. He doubted if he was the only cop a little lit. As Harry stepped onto the detective floor, one of the vice cops grabbed him and said, "You had better follow us, we're heading to the briefing room for our assignments."

A sea of loose ties, fedoras and crumpled shirts made their way into a square-shaped room cluttered with uncomfortable wooden chairs. At the front of the room was a stand. Harry took a seat somewhere near the middle of the room and slouched into the chair. He expected Carter or another department head to walk in; instead, he scoffed and moaned along with many other detectives when Lionel Beek stepped through the door and took his place proudly behind the stand.

"Good afternoon, ladies and gentlemen," Beek said, "I appreciate you all coming in at a short notice. Now, I am sure many of you are concerned for your colleagues who are currently unaccounted for. I assure you we are doing what we can to establish their whereabouts and make contact with them."

"What are you doing?" an elderly detective asked, one who was probably close to claiming his pension and cared little for brass bullshit.

"I am sorry, I don't understand the question," Beek said. He continued shuffling a bundle of papers nervously and cleared his throat repeatedly.

"You said you are doing what you can. What is that exactly?"

"We are going to send a hazmat team into the undercity to see what the situation is down there. Hopefully we can establish contact with someone down there."

"You'll only find bodies!" another detective shouted.

A detective sitting behind Harry agreed and said, "Yeah, haven't you heard from the poor folk down there? They talk about people hitting the deck after breathing in a single mouthful of that stuff! What chance do our boys have down there? Hell, the Black Lungs got a better chance than they do. They are probably picking the bones of our boys clean as we sit on our asses!"

Whispers were now being shared in the room, the rumblings of sighs and complaints began to get louder and louder until Beek decided enough was enough.

"Alright. Settle down. Settle down!" he shouted, trying to command some respect in the room.

"Look, I get it, ok, nobody has any real answers yet, right now I need to give out your assignments and you need to do your jobs. Everyone's cases will be put on hold. You'll be assigned new duties. Now listen up."

Beek rattled off a list of names and announced their new assignments. Some with given close protection duties for high-risk targets such as affluent businessmen who had likely made hefty donations to the force over the years or were cosy with the mayor or commissioner. Others were assigned zones to investigate any cult activity that had been rumoured to be going on. Mainly in the derelict towers or ones that were in a state of disrepair. Not many of these buildings still stood in the city. If there was an empty building, it meant less property taxes and they were quickly refurbished and inhabited.

Harry and two other detectives were assigned to investigate the top floors of The Wilbur Building. It had sustained severe damage when a cargo plane had malfunctioned and crashed into it a few months ago. Its peak had been decimated and now a huge hole stood in its place. It was due a massive renovation once a contract had been agreed. A police blimp had reported seeing unusual activity inside the crater earlier that night.

"Hey Beek!" the detective sat next to Harry shouted. "Where are you getting these places from anyway? Nobody has lived in some of these buildings for months, they are derelict shitholes full of squatters who have snuck up from the undercity."

"The commissioner and the department heads are concerned that these are the sort of places the children will be operating from. Some uniforms have even said they have spotted what looks like one or two members knocking around those parts. Just go there, see what you can find and report back. The rest of you have your principals you need to protect."

"Don't they have their own damn private security?!" Another detective towards the back of the room shouted.

"They do, but given the heightened threat level, they will now receive police protection."

"Why? They weren't the ones who had their homes gassed. I don't see any of them dead on the streets."

Several shouts of 'yeah!' and 'that's right!' erupted in the stuffy room. Harry had managed to bite his tongue the entire time but was also losing his patience.

"Look, just do what is asked of you. You will all be suitably compensated when you file your overtime reports. Now, do I have any more questions?"

"What do we do if we find any cultists?" a female detective asked, the first woman to shout up since everyone had entered the room.

"The mayor has ordered a shoot-to-kill order."

"What?!" Harry shouted. "This isn't a war zone, we aren't hitmen. We need to arrest and interrogate them. Try and get some information out of them and hopefully one or two of the lesser committed will break and tell us their next move."

Several cheers and shouts of approval were heard across the room.

"I get your concern, Detective, but the mayor has deemed all cultists to be a threat to the city, and they are too dangerous to be left alive. Even though I myself managed to get Jasper Volster to confess to his father's murder, the city officials do not want to take any more chances. Jasper is to be executed tomorrow evening."

"In front of a mass audience, I assume?" Harry said, sitting upright in the uncomfortable hard chair. He knew Beek couldn't resist gloating about what was likely a bullshit confession.

"Yes. Why?"

"Great idea, get thousands of people together in one place, see how well that goes. It'll be a cultists' wet dream, you buffoon!"

The room erupted again with shouts of support for Harry. Beek had lost the room and started to feel small.

He frantically fiddled with the sheets of paper in front of him and cleared his throat again.

"I will…I will raise your concerns to the commissioner. Now…uh…dismissed…all of you!"

The several dozen detectives who had squeezed themselves into the small and stuffy room stood up to take their leave. Nearly everyone stared at Beek disapprovingly as they exited the room. Beek, who was too afraid to look at any of them, continued to fiddle with his notes until the room emptied.

Harry walked back towards his desk and was followed by Detectives Edward Lock and Viggo Thorne. Both worked homicide and the three knew each other fairly well.

They all had a similar time on the job as Harry and shared a dislike for the rodent who had just given them their orders. Lock often favoured white or light grey suits and hats which looked sharp against his dark, olive skin. He was stylistic, tall and often drew the gaze from the ladies. Thorne was shorter and broader, who cared little for whatever suit he pulled out of his wardrobe. He was a devoted family man who took as many extra shifts as he could to pay for his wife's cancer treatment. Both were good dependable cops.

"What are they expecting us to find up there?" Lock asked, pulling a cigarette out from a tin and offering one to Harry and Thorne.

Thorne declined and said, "I don't even know if it's safe to enter. That plane did some serious damage; I look at the hole every day I drive to work."

Harry chose to remain silent and listened to the concerns and frustrations of his colleagues. He would usually agree with them, but the cult had gone to certain lengths to keep their whereabouts a secret. An abandoned and potentially dangerous tower would make sense if they didn't want to be found.

"Harry," Lock said, offering him a cigarette. "You've dealt with these robe-wearing freaks before. What can we expect?"

Harry accepted the cigarette from Lock and struck a match from a box he had lying on his desk. He lit the cigarette, took a drag and said, "They are dangerous and deluded, we can't take any chances."

Thorne and Lock looked at one another and simultaneously said, "Shotguns."

CHAPTER TWENTY

Harry followed the two detectives out of the armoury, each pointing the barrel of their pump actions in the air. They almost seemed excited, like they were preparing to go on a long hunt to hopefully return with glorious trophies and stories of courage and valour.

"Harry," Carter said, catching up with them in the corridor, "you got a minute?"

His armpits were stained with sweat, and he looked as if he hadn't changed his shirt in days judging by the amount of different coloured food stains it had just beneath the collar.

"Now who looks like shit," Harry joked. Hoping his supervisor would see the funny side for once. He didn't mention the repulsive body odour.

"Now aint the time, son. I haven't spoken to you properly since you got back from the undercity. I didn't even know you were alive until a beat cop told me he saw you slip out the building during all the madness."

"Yeah, look, sorry, Chief. There was a lot going on that day. I know I should have checked in but…"

"I should be the one apologising to you."

"Sir?"

It was rare for a man of Carter's character to apologise or admit he was wrong. He was strong willed and stubborn, typical of many senior cops.

"You told me about the attack, and I didn't do enough to look into it. A lot of this is on me."

"Don't do that to yourself, David," Harry said, the hypocrisy not wasted on himself.

"Either way, I am sorry. I should have trusted you. Volster and a couple other big-time firms are sending teams down there tomorrow morning to assess the damage, a couple support cops are going down with them just in case."

"Well, let's hope some people made it to higher ground."

"You find out anything else you tell me; this time I promise you: I'll do something about it."

" I discovered the cult's boss's hideout. It was in a bunker beneath a farmhouse, way out in the dustbowl. A place called Proctor's Farm past a small town called Bonesville, this was where Jasper sent me."

"Leave it with me, I'll notify the feds and get them to send a team out there."

"Alright. Hopefully they have more luck than I did. Tell them to touch base with Sheriff Miles, the local lawman out there, he can point them in the right direction."

"Ok."

"Oh, and tell them, they'll need to bring a truck or something. The Leader…the chief cultist or whatever he is. He…he's on some sort of life support machine. I aint ever seen anything like it before."

"Leave it with me, be safe out there. I am glad to see you are taking extra precautions." David glanced at the shotgun and then took his leave.

"Harry!" Lock shouted. "You coming or what?!"

The highway which led to The Wilbur Building had been blocked off by a metal gate which prevented access to the public. Thorne had the code, so he unlocked it and drove the trio through towards the building's car port. They took his car as it was the only one that was big enough to transport the three of them. Like Harry, Lock enjoyed roadsters and drove a classic which even Harry was envious of. Unlike the rest of the towers which glowed brightly in the night sky, The Wilbur was shrouded in darkness, save for the odd flicker of light which were likely from the squatters who had moved into the abandoned tower. The building once sported a distinct patterned dome on its peak where the penthouse had been. Now a crater took its place, caused by the downed plane. Only the southern portion of the dome remained. The aircraft had been removed; however, work had yet to begin on the repairs to the rest of the building. Harry looked straight up at the damage which glowed when a police blimp stuck its spotlight on it.

"Well," Lock said, "I don't think the lifts are going to work. Let's talk to some of the residents, see if they have seen any of our friends about."

"I should have worn more comfortable shoes today," Thorne complained, working out how many flights of stairs he'd have to climb to reach the top.

Most of the apartments had been locked tight with heavy metal doors, the ones that weren't had been looted and stripped. As the detectives stepped onto the last floor just below the demolished penthouse, they spotted something scurrying in the shadows.

"What the fuck was that?" a startled Thorne said, racking his shotgun and pointing it into the dark abyss.

Lock placed his hand gently on the barrel, lowered it and said, "Relax, I think it was just a kid."

The hallway was dark except for the glow of candles that were dotted about the place. Some of the apartments had squatters living in them who shielded themselves from the gaze of the detectives under blankets and newspapers as they walked past.

"Guessing the locals are afraid we are here to turf them out," Thorne said.

"Wouldn't you be?" Lock said. "This is probably the best they've ever had it, even if it is inside a building which could crumble at any moment."

A young child covered in dirt stepped out of the shadows and stared at the detectives. They stood silently and stared back at the skinny child who wore rags for clothes. He was barefoot and clearly malnourished.

"Hey there, fella," Harry said softly. "What's your name?"

The kid didn't reply, although he smiled at Harry who took a knee.

"You hungry?"

Harry grabbed a candy bar out of the inside of his coat pocket and reached out towards the child. The boy took a few steps forward and extended his arm.

"Ah," Harry said, pulling his hand backwards away from the boy who froze in disappointment.

"First, I need you to tell me if you have seen some people here. Some new people. Can you do that for me?"

The boy nodded; he still hadn't made a sound since he'd appeared before the detectives.

"Have you seen some new people here? Bald heads, red long robes Look like this fella?" Harry held up Jasper Volster's mugshot towards the child.

He nodded and pointed his index finger towards the ceiling.

"The penthouse?"

The boy nodded.

"Thanks kids, I owe you one." He handed the child the candy bar who snatched it from his grasp and scurried off into the darkness not to be seen again.

The detectives crept through the rest of the corridor until they reached the stairs which led to the penthouse, the door was locked so Thorne and Lock kicked it open. They doubted the stairs were ever used but given that the power was out, the elevator wasn't an option. As they stepped onto the penthouse floor, the wind whistled through what was once a sumptuous living space. The large crater looked out onto the dozens of illuminated buildings standing tall. Most of the furniture had been smashed to pieces, a bookcase had toppled over, and what books that hadn't been destroyed in the crash had been ruined by the weather. The detectives walked out onto a metal walkway. Staircases on either side led down onto the main floor.

"I don't think anybody is living here," Lock said. "I mean how could they? Place is a total mess. Sky boys have gotten it wrong again."

"Let's at least look around before we call it a night," Harry said, splitting off from the other two and taking the far set of stairs.

The metal creaked under his footsteps, and he hoped they were still sturdy enough to hold his weight. He was relieved when he stepped onto the floor and heard the sound of shattered glass crunching beneath his shoes. The sound of the wind gave the place an eerie feeling. During the last week, Harry had found himself in more uncomfortable environments than he usually would in a whole year on the job. He knelt down and picked up a cracked photo frame and examined a weathered photo of an attractive man and woman. He presumed they were the penthouse's inhabitants who had tragically lost their lives when the plane came down. He didn't know their names nor what they had done to be able to afford this once magnificent home. Both Lock and Thorne pushed around debris and ripped open drawers from broken cabinets, looking for anything of interest. Harry stepped towards the enormous hole and admired the view.

"Jeez, Harry, you aint thinking of jumping, are you?" Lock said jovially.

Harry looked over at his colleague and smiled. His expression then turned to one of panic as he observed a hooded figure emerging from the darkness. The figure drove a knife into his fellow detective's chest. Lock fell to the floor and began coughing blood. Thorne took aim with his shotgun and blew the attacker back into the shadows where they crashed against a side table.

"Lock! Fuck!" Thorne screamed, taking a knee beside his colleague and grabbing his hand. The wounded detective coughed blood onto Thorne's shirt and writhed until he lay his head back onto the floor. He tried to speak, but every time he did, he just coughed more blood.

"I'll get you out of here, buddy, just hang on. Harry, give me a hand here, will you?" Thorne said. His voice full of fear and panic.

Harry dropped the shotgun onto the floor and went to lift the wounded officer to his feet. Once he was up, they turned towards the stairs to make their escape. Another cultist appeared out of the shadows ahead of them, holding a curved knife. They lunged towards the trio. Harry didn't have time to reach for the shotgun which he had left on the floor; instead, his hand reached for his revolver. It had barely cleared the holster as the cultist's blade reached for Thorne's neck. One. Two. Three. Harry fired rapid shots from the hip and the cultist went down with an almighty thud.

Lowering his piece, Harry said, "We've gotta get out of here now." Thorne dragged Lock towards the stairs. As he went to lift his wounded friend onto the first step, he felt a sudden sharp pain in his chest. Thorne looked down to see a knife protruding from his sternum, it had sliced his tie clean in half. He dropped to the floor and Lock fell on top of him, both lifeless.

Harry didn't see who had thrown the knife; he fired blindly into the darkness, hoping to kill whoever it belonged to. The flash from his short muzzle briefly illuminated the black void although he still didn't see the attacker. When his revolver ran dry, he swung the cylinder open and scrambled to release the spent cases. As the last one dropped to the floor, he reached into his coat pocket to grab hold of as many loose rounds as he could. The attacker appeared before him again and raised his arm. Yet another bald figure in a red robe. Harry ducked to the right as a blade cut through the darkness towards his face, narrowly missing his ear by inches. As he crashed onto the debris-ridden floor, the revolver fell from his grasp and slid under a heavy chunk of concrete. Both he and the cultist clocked the shotgun a couple of feet ahead of them and both made a grab for it. Harry lunged forward on his knees, needing to retrieve it before the murderer standing next to him did. He wasn't fast enough; the cultist swiped it from the two fingers he had managed to grab it with and raised the barrel towards his face as he knelt on the filthy floor. The cultist pulled the trigger, but nothing happened. He pulled it again and again yet still there was no loud bang or explosion of fire and smoke. Quickly realising that the cultist didn't know how to work the safety, he used the opportunity to gain the advantage. Dragging himself to his feet, he pushed the barrel away and threw a punch towards the cultist. He landed a hard one square on his nose that sent him stumbling backwards. They let go of the shotgun which landed onto some smashed picture frames. Droplets of blood escaped their nose and began to fall onto the dusty ground. The cultist wiped his nose, smearing the blood across his dry lips. He showed a panicked Harry a deathly smile and placed the tip of his knife against his scarred lips and wiped some of the blood away. Another ex-fumer. Harry dropped to his knees again and grabbed the shotgun, he raised it horizontally above his head and blocked the blade as it came crashing down towards his face. All he had to do was get one good shot off and the fight would be over. He pushed himself backwards off his knees and back up onto his feet. The floor was slippery due to all the rubble, dust and debris. Harry took two steps backwards and raised the shotgun again, but the cultist was too quick. He ducked below the barrel and pushed it away as Harry slipped the safety off and squeezed the trigger. The kick sent him another step backwards, dangerously close to the edge of the crater. He felt the ground beneath his right foot give way and he nearly fell to his doom. He scrambled forward trying to find firmer footing and fell right into the cultist's boot. A sharp pain ran across his right cheek followed by the taste of blood again in his mouth. The cultist slashed at Harry who leapt backwards and narrowly avoided being disembowelled. The blade sliced a good length of Harry's tie off. He racked the shotgun again and placed it against his hip, hoping to squeeze off another shot and at least clip the cultist. The cultist lunged forward as Harry fired. Buckshot tore through his left thigh as he let out a piercing scream and fell to the floor. Harry stepped around the cultist who had his back inches from the edge of the crater. Another shell hit the floor as Harry racked the shotgun and placed it into his shoulder. He had a clean shot and could blow this son of a bitch back down into the undercity.

"Wait…" the cultist said, turning his attention from his bloodied thigh towards Harry.

"Are you really going to beg me for your life? After what you just did!?"

"Oh no, detective, not at all. I just wanted to make sure you didn't miss tonight's firework display." The cultist kept looking behind him, towards the glowing buildings.

"What fucking fireworks? What the hell are you talking about?!" Harry said, taking a small step forward, his finger resting against the trigger.

The cultist reached into his robe and retrieved a bundle of cylinders that had been taped together. Wires protruded from their tips and ran into what looked like some sort of electronic device that had a small red light attached to it. It took but a second for Harry to realise it was a bomb and he contemplated his next move. He couldn't risk firing and denotating it. But he also couldn't risk letting the cultist do it themselves and blow them both and every squatter to smithereens.

"And what are you going to do with that?" Harry asked. He wanted to bide some time whilst he figured out what to do next.

"Any moment now," the cultist said, looking over his shoulder again.

A low humming noise could be heard, which soon became louder and louder. Harry's eyes widened as he realised what the cultist had planned.

He lowered the shotgun and stepped forward, hoping to snatch the bomb out of the cultist's hand and prayed it wouldn't detonate. The cultist smiled at Harry as he staggered backwards, extended his arms and pushed himself off the edge of the building. Harry froze until the view of the city was blocked as a blimp raised itself above him. He could almost touch it as it made its ascension above the ruined tower. The following explosion deafened him as he scrambled to take cover. All the helium inside of the blimp ignited and the flames began to spread across its frame. Harry was powerless to watch as it drifted back down towards the fog. The thumps of four other explosions echoed throughout the city. Another ball of fire could be seen in the distance between a pair of towers. They had struck again, this time directly at those who were meant to maintain law and order. Two detectives lay dead behind Harry, and God knows how many more officers had perished in those blimps. Harry slumped to the floor, defeated. Doubt began to creep into his mind. No matter what he did, or tried to do, they were always a step ahead of him and didn't care who they hurt, nor how.

It was daylight before the body collectors arrived to retrieve the corpses. Harry insisted that neither Lock nor Thorne rode in the same truck as the psychopaths. The collector told him of several other attacks that night, cop ambushes and explosions. One of the blimps had crashed near a refugee centre but by some miracle had only scorched the paving. Every cop in the blimp perished though. It was pandemonium out there and the military couldn't arrive any sooner. Harry rummaged through the remains of the destroyed penthouse, hoping to find a clue or something that would alert him to the cult's next target. Before the body collector zipped the bag, Harry searched through the cultist's robes and found a handful of paper envelopes. Most contained flyers and cryptic messages he had already seen. Although, one appeared to be a sketch of a seating plan of some kind. Its layout reminded Harry of a theatre. Most were being used to house refugees and would make good targets. Some of the seats were numbered from one to five.

After stuffing the paper into his coat pocket, he took hold of Thorne's car keys. He would break the news to his wife himself later that morning.

***

Orson Oldfield was the most junior member of the Volster hazardous materials team. He had only been on the job a month, and he was nervous that his first assignment was inspecting the undercity. Unlike the other teams, they had no police support as they were stretched thin and his supervisor had told Orson this would be a quick job – in and out were the words used.

His supervisor had also ensured him that the clunky and stuffy hazmat suit he was wearing would protect him from the zeron gas that still lingered in the dark streets. If it didn't, he would be dead within seconds of the elevator door opening. His suit was bright yellow. Attached to the front were a group of pouches containing different tools and anti-toxins. The heavy duty gas mask obscured his vision, and it was hard to see out of. On his back was a weighty power pack which could be used by a variety of machinery the team brought with them. Orson rode the elevator all the way into the undercity. It was cramped; three of his colleagues stood behind him, hunched together. It was also dark, save for the blue glow of their power packs. He wanted to adjust his mask, but he was terrified he would break a seal and be dead as soon as the doors opened. He couldn't feel much in his thick rubber gloves anyway, so he let it be.

"You good, kid?" a muffled voice said behind him.

Orson tried to twist his neck but could only move it a couple of inches; he chose to raise his thumb and then turned to face the elevator doors again. They were using a small maintenance lift which was hidden away. He doubted if the police even knew of its existence.

The elevator slowed and then stopped. Orson pulled a lever, and the doors separated. Visibility was almost non-existent. It was as if the fog had lowered itself and now consumed everything it touched. "Let's go," another muffled voice said.

Orson felt himself being pushed into a small alleyway. He didn't know where he was but that didn't matter. All he had to do was take a couple of samples and be out of there. The group turned left and walked through the narrow alley towards a street. Orson stumbled over something and panicked when he saw the corpse of a woman. Her face was blistered, and her skin was a greeny-grey colour.

"Come on," Orson's supervisor said. "There are plenty more up here."

Orson turned around to see a break in the fog. The street ahead of him was littered with corpses, similar in appearance to the woman by his feet. It was like something out of a war documentary. Until this day, Orson had never seen a dead body, and now he had seen more than many would in a lifetime.

The hazmat team made their way down the street, trying not to trip over the bodies which lay in their way. A bead of sweat ran down his face, but he couldn't do anything about it. The sweat distracted him momentarily until he heard a noise, like a whip cracking through the air. The man ahead of him fell onto his front and didn't get back up. Another crack, this time the man behind him fell.

"Orson." A muffled voice shouted. "Run!"

Doing just this, he didn't stop or turn to look back, he couldn't, not with the mask on. He ran past his colleague and heard many more cracks. He didn't hear the final one until he was already falling to the floor. He lay on his side, breathing sharply. He could feel the life draining from his body. Out of the fog walked three monstrous figures, clad in a frightening breathing apparatus, almost like a demonic version of their own. The pumps on their back raised and lowered with a loud, sharp hiss. The demon raised the barrel of the pistol, and Orson took solace in the fact that he would soon be out of this horrible suit forever.

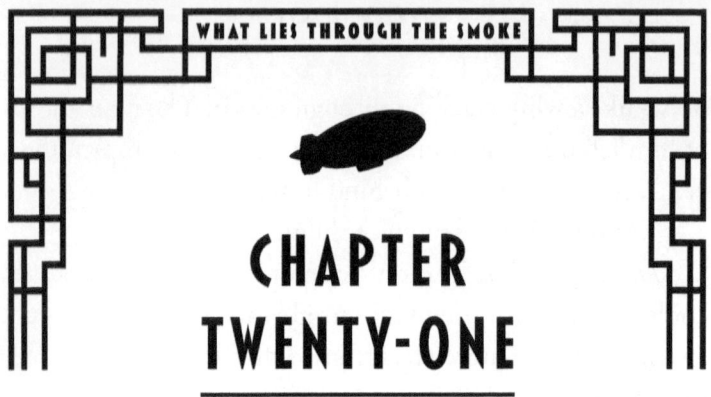

CHAPTER TWENTY-ONE

ionel Beek stood talking to two junior patrolmen. Nodding, listening intensely to every word he said, not experienced enough to see through the bullshit that escaped his mouth. Anyone who knew Beek avoided him like the plague except those who were forced to keep his company. Even the commissioner knew he was a suck up, but he was a useful suck up at that. Harry stepped off the elevator with two other detectives. One with a bandage around his forehead. He and his partner had narrowly avoided being chopped to pieces when they were sent to investigate an abandoned food processing plant. They had shot one cultist dead, but four others got away. It was turmoil out there. More cops had been killed in the last week than in the last five years. Hopefully, once the military arrived, they would have a fighting chance. It wasn't as if the cultists were better equipped – most of them didn't carry firearms. But, they were fearless, determined and unrelenting in their dedication to violence and death. Harry couldn't remember the last time the city had faced a crisis like this. The status quo was shifting. For a long time the city had been delicately balanced, the police did what they had to do to stop the city from imploding and destroying itself. The criminals walked a similar line, knowing that without some order there would be no way to run their enterprises. Anarchy suited nobody, and that was exactly what was happening right now. Harry was furious and felt as if his blood was almost literally boiling. He saw Beek with his pathetic childlike face and then saw nothing but red. The two patrolmen were bemused when a grizzled homicide detective dragged Beek across the room and threw him across a desk, spilling a mountain of paperwork onto the worn carpet. Beek struggled to get to his feet, but Harry held him down and began to choke him with his own expensive silk tie. Beek tried to speak, but all he could muster was a gargle as his face reddened.

Pressing his face against Beek's, Harry snarled, "You are sending officers to their death, you piece of shit. Why don't you get out on the streets and see what it's like out there!"

Nobody intervened, most stood and watched in pure jealousy as Beek finally took what had been coming to him for years.

"That's enough, Harry," a voice said.

Ignoring it, savouring the moment. "Quinn! That's enough!"

Harry looked up to see both Carter and Commissioner Harris watching the fiasco. He turned his gaze back to Beek who was clenching his teeth and trying to wiggle himself free. Harry released the weasel of a man and stepped away from him.

Beek shot up and loosened his tie. He took a deep breath and sheepishly said, "I want that man arrested. You two, arrest him." Beek looked at the two junior patrolmen he had been talking to who were stood doing nothing.

"Shut the hell up, Beek, get out of this office," Commissioner Harris said.

Beek looked over at the man he had spent months running around after, eager to please in total disbelief.

"Sir?" he muttered in bewilderment.

"Now, Beek!" Harris said, pointing towards the door.

Beek stood up and scurried away, yearning to be clear of the many pairs of eyes that stared at him with total hatred and disrespect.

Harry brushed himself down and adjusted his clothes.

"You want my badge, sir?" he said.

"Absolutely not," Harris said. "Follow me."

Harry followed Carter and Harris into his supervisor's office. He shut the door behind him and Carter tilted the blinds.

Harris turned and said, "Beek has had that coming for years. He will be reassigned where he can't do any more damage. Perhaps logistic supply or uniform stores. I am sorry to hear what happened out there. It's pure horror. Every cop is being called in. Even those who have recently retired are being asked to take up the badge again. We need all the help we can get."

"What's next, sir? We keep hunting the cult while they keep hunting us?"

"No. Support units will now be conducting the raids on the hideouts. Jasper Volster is going to be executed tomorrow at noon. It's going to be public and despite me making my concerns clear to the mayor, he and the other city officials have insisted they want it witnessed in front of the city."

"It's insane, sir, why is nobody listening to us?"

"Because they never have, Harry. This city doesn't belong to us. It never has. We are simply a force to be used and played with when the city sees fit. I don't need to tell you how deep the corruption runs. I have done what I can in my tenure as commissioner, but I fear nothing will ever be enough. The mayor knows it, and that is why he has asked me to step down after the execution."

"What?"

"Yes, he has lined up a replacement, someone who he says is more agreeable."

"What are you going to do?"

"Find a hat and a pair of more comfortable shoes. It's been a long time since I worked the streets of this city, and I want it to know I am still a police officer."

"What happens next?"

"Everyone will be given their assignments for the executions tomorrow. Jasper and the other imprisoned cultists are going to be hanged in a plaza. The place is going to be crawling with officials, bigwigs and tower dwellers, but also the displaced. The mayor wants the refugees to see it as a warning, so they aren't tempted down the same path."

"It'll be crawling with cultists also."

"It will, and what's concerning is some of our cops that have ended up dead have had their uniforms stolen."

"You're kidding?"

"We suspect they will be masquerading as us, to get close to their targets."

"Godammit. We aren't going to know who is who."

"We aren't. You're right."

"Is there any news on the undercity? Did the hazmat teams come up with anything?"

"They tried but it seems the Black Lungs haven't taken kindly to anyone invading their new kingdom. It turns out their vulgar technology stops zeron gas. We managed to make contact with a few squads of officers who had made it to higher ground when the bombs went off. They are held up in apartment buildings, trying to keep a low profile. The Black Lungs are on the hunt and have asserted dominance in many sectors. Their competition, the Junkers, have almost been wiped out. I hope when the military arrives tomorrow, they are going to take the fight to them and take the streets back. I have been told Volster is going to test out a gas which should hopefully neutralize zeron and make the streets safe again."

"Is it that simple?"

"I hope so. Although everything is theoretical at the moment. Sadly, I won't be told anymore now."

"I understand, sir."

"Harry," Carter said. "How did Thorne's wife take the news?"

"About as good as any loving wife could. She burst into tears and chain-smoked the whole time I was there."

"I'll make sure every family is compensated. The mayor can dig into his own pockets if he has to," Harris said. "I may no longer be the commissioner, but I'll do what I can to help, even if it isn't much."

"Take a break, Harry," Carter said. "Take a shower and get something to eat."

"You got it."

Harry could feel himself shaking and wasn't against the idea of getting some chow. Long hours, too much coffee and smoking wasn't good for anyone, and he needed to stay sharp. As he shut Carter's door, he noticed Victoria stood in the middle of the detective's floor. For the first time in many years, the cigarette haze had vanished, given how few officers were sitting at their desks. Like Harry, those that remained stared at and admired the beautiful redhead who stood looking lost like a stray cat. She was the best thing he had seen all day, and he smiled as they locked eyes with one another. Victoria stomped towards him and wrapped her arms around his body. The other detectives, disappointed, went back to their work.

"It's good to see you," Harry said, lowering his hands to her waist.

"Likewise, I saw the attacks on the blimps, I was so worried about you. You didn't call."

"I'm sorry, a lot has been going on."

"I know it has. My brother has made a deal with the mayor to start decontaminating the undercity once the army arrive. The company had developed a way of neutralizing zeron gas shortly after it was banned. They've lost survey teams to the gangs down there and can't risk losing anymore. How are things your end?"

"Not good, we are losing cops by the minute. We have been told to shoot cultists on sight. Those that are in custody are going to be executed tomorrow, along with your brother."

"Can I see him?"

"Is that a good idea?"

"I don't know, but this is likely going to be my last opportunity. I need to…I need to see him with my own eyes; he was always a terrible liar."

"I shouldn't. But I know what you are feeling. Come on, follow me."

Harry escorted Victoria down to the cell blocks which were brimming with prisoners. The cultists had been given their own cell towards the far end of the room so they couldn't be injured by makeshift missiles from the other residents who didn't take too kindly to their presence. The other cell blocks were full of those who had escaped the undercity. Many had been arrested for petty thefts and burglaries. Some had used the opportunity to try and make some extra cash, the others were just desperate.

"You sure about this, Detective?" the guard asked. "I don't want to remind you what happened last time. He has already confessed to that other cop."

"Please, I won't be the one talking to him," Harry said.

The guard looked at Victoria and said, "Who is she?"

"A consultant."

Victoria remained silent and simply nodded.

"Alright. But if anything happens, I'll have to report it."

"Of course, thanks."

The guard led the pair down the long wing until they came to the cell where a dozen cultists sat in silence. Jasper sat on a bunk leaning his head against the wall. He saw Victoria and his eyes widened.

"Ah. Dear sister!" he said excitedly, "It has been too long. Why has it taken you this long to visit me?"

"Jasper," Victoria said, emotionless. "Let's talk."

"Indeed, let us."

The way he spoke made her skin crawl. She could just about tolerate him being a junkie, but now his mind had been twisted and warped, and he was too far gone.

"Step towards the door," the guard said.

Once Jasper was handcuffed and out of the cell, he was escorted towards an interview room. Jeers and insults were expressed by the other prisoners who didn't take kindly to seeing a cultist walking past their cells. He maintained a faint smile and kept his head low.

"Not exactly going to plan, is it?" Harry said. "The masses aren't being rallied, they aren't rising up and taking this city back like you and your thugs imagined. They are afraid and angry. Angry at you and your sick group."

"Time will tell, Detective. It didn't take much to destabilize the city, did it? Simply drag a few thousand extra people out of the depths, kill a few police officers and the city dropped onto its knees. They will look to those who can provide them with a brighter future."

"Somehow I don't think they will take kindly to those who murdered their families."

"Time will tell."

Jasper was placed back into an interview room, Victoria followed him inside and told Harry to wait in the other room, behind the two-way mirror. Jasper would know he was there, but he didn't care.

"It is nice to see you, sister; it has been a while."

"I wish I could say the same," Victoria said, taking a seat at the table opposite her brother. "What is the endgame,

Jasper? We thought it was the gas, but clearly that was just the beginning. What are you and your gang planning?"

"If I told you, it would ruin the surprise."

"Goddammit, Jasper. You spent your whole life rebelling against authority, against our father, and yet now, for some reason, you choose to blindly follow this group. Why?"

"Because they are finally the ones who will save this city. Our father, and many like him, simply wanted to control it. To bend it to their will and rape it, just like Horus does."

Victoria shook at the thought of her brother's touch. She composed herself and said, "Our father never stopped loving you, Jasper. He told me many times that he wanted you back with us. He took the blame for failing you, for allowing you to sink deeper and deeper into that hole you found yourself in. It broke his heart every time he saw you. You looked worse each visit."

Jasper started to become agitated at the thought. He hadn't felt any feelings towards his father for years.

"Our father was the very thing wrong with this city, and you know this. His heart was as black as exhaust smoke. Many more like him are going to die. And then maybe this city will have a chance."

"When?"

"Wait, my dear sister. Wait and your patience will be rewarded."

"How did they get to you, Jasper? The cult I mean?"

"They found us."

"Fumers?"

"Yes. They found us and offered us a solution. We were given an opportunity to be reborn. Given another chance."

"How many of you are there? Really?"

"Even I don't know the exact number. But it doesn't matter if you kill every last one of us. Our teachings will be followed for years now."

"So, you kill every rich person in this city? Then what? Your leader going to strap on a suit and run for mayor? Are you going to set up your own political party, perhaps run for presidency? What exactly do you think is going to happen, Jasper? The city won't change. It never will. It simply just is what it is. It's its own creature, it has a soul."

"We shall see tomorrow."

"Is that when the next attack will be? During your execution?"

"Like I said, I don't want to ruin the surprise."

Jasper pressed his index finger against his lips and leant back into his chair.

"Why did you tell them you killed Dad?"

"Because, your poor friend Harry has worked so hard and yielded such little results. Besides, you know who did, don't you, sister?"

Victoria looked away from her brother. Before she could answer, the door burst open and a uniformed officer dashed inside, revolver in hand and pointed it at Jasper. He pulled the trigger and painted the room with fragments of Jasper's blood and skull. Harry watched from the other side of the mirror and sprinted out of the room. The officer turned his gaze to Victoria who sat in fright, covered in her brother's brain matter.

"Put the gun down! Now!" Harry shouted from the doorway as he held his revolver towards the manic officer.

The officer dropped the gun to the floor and fell to his knees. Without being ordered, he placed his hands across the back of his head and allowed Harry to cuff him. Two other officers sprinted into the room, both clutching their guns. They escorted him out of the room as Harry tended to Victoria.

"Are you ok?" he asked.

"I...I think so, my god. His blood is all over me. Was that...was that..."

"A cultist? No... I have seen him before. Geez what the hell is going on?"

Harry looked over at Jasper's lifeless body as it slumped in the chair. Blood dripped from the hole in the back of his skull.

"Come on, let's get you out of this room."

CHAPTER
TWENTY-TWO

It transpired that the officer who murdered Jasper had witnessed his partner being stabbed to death earlier that morning. They had been sent to investigate a cult sighting inside a rail tunnel. His partner of five years, who also happened to be his brother-in-law, had taken a blade to the neck from a cultist when they came across their hideout. By the time the officer had dragged his partner out of the tunnel he had already bled out. The cultist had escaped, and the officer wanted to satisfy his lust for revenge. When he heard from the jail guard that Jasper Volster was out of his cell, he had taken his opportunity to exert some payback, no matter what it would cost him. The police were exhausted and paranoid and had little left to give. Mistakes were being made, and lives were being lost. Harry drove Victoria back to his place where she showered and scrubbed the remains of her brother off her face and out of her hair. Harry could hear her sobbing as the water cut off so he figured it would be a good idea to pour her a glass of whisky. She came out wearing just a towel and leant against the door to his living room.

"Here," Harry said as he handed her the glass. She took it from him and downed it in one gulp. "You want another one?"

"Sure. Thanks."

Harry had a couple of hours' respite before Carter needed him back at the precinct so he could brief what was left of the force before the executions took place. Despite Jasper having bought it back at the precinct, the other cultists were to be put to death in front of a bloodthirsty mob. It was a bad idea and every cop knew it.

"You not having one?" Victoria asked.

"No, I'm needed back soon. Did you get anywhere with Horus?"

"He was busy with emergency board meetings. I managed to release more funds for food rations. I have also requested more supplies to the police, hospitals and fire services. You should hopefully see Volster tech arriving at your place."

"Great, we need all the help we can get now."

Harry poured the last of the whisky bottle into the glass and returned to Victoria.

She took hold of it and quietly said, "I know. God, things have changed so quickly, Harry."

"Something is going to happen at the execution," she continued, "I know it."

"Everyone does. The stupidity of this city knows no bounds. All we can do is wait and see."

"Please be careful."

"I want you to stay here."

"I can't, the company wants me back at the tower before the execution, there is going to be a meeting afterwards with the city's officials and other companies."

"Where is this meeting taking place?"

"No idea, it's being kept a secret, I suppose they are afraid as well."

"As soon as you find out let me know."

"I will."

It was eight in the morning when Harry took his seat in the briefing room along with the other detectives. There were fewer than the day before, some hadn't returned from their assignments and there was a sombre feeling in the air. Everyone looked tired, downtrodden and defeated. Several patrolmen stood at the back of the room. Their uniforms were crinkled, stained and their boots were scuffed. They had probably been on duty for hours already and had little left to give. Commissioner Harris walked into the room sporting a burgundy suit with a white shirt, black tie and matching hat. The man clearly had taste when he didn't have to wear bureaucratic apparel. Beek was absent , and nobody missed him. The other department heads followed. Carter had freshened up and changed his suit.

"Good morning, ladies and gentlemen," Commissioner Harris said.

"I regret to inform you that today will be my last day as your commissioner. My last job in the role is to brief you on today's events. Although I'll still be your ground commander."

Whispers and dull chatter filled the room. Harry remained silent and watched as Harris gripped the stand. Each officer was given their post. The executions were due to take place in a plaza outside of City Hall. The city's officials would watch from a series of balconies. Snipers were being positioned around the towers to keep an overwatch on the proceedings. Three strong lines of heavily armoured support officers would stand between the sentenced cultists and the crowd to ensure the proceedings went smoothly. Harry was assigned to stand guard by City Hall's entrance and observe the crowd. The buildings had been searched far and wide for any zeron gas canisters or anything suspicious. It had been deemed all clear and was now packed with important figureheads. Every officer took advantage of the charitable donations from Volster and other companies, and loaded up with modern military grade lightweight body armour, powerful semi-automatic pistols and handheld radios which were heavy and clumsy to use.

The plaza was rammed with people, probably more than it had ever seen. At the front, by the entrance to City Hall, were the condemned, stood with their hands bound on the gallows. The crowd goers stared at them intensely. Some with hatred, others with pity. A speaker system had been set up, and the announcer started to read the names of the cultists who stood perfectly still with ropes around their necks. None flinched nor moved. They seem totally unfazed about their impending demise. Harry stood on the stairs by the entrance and paced nervously. His radio was alive with transmissions from command staff and the officers on overwatch. He looked at the windows of the surrounding towers and spotted a couple of sniper teams who sported fancy new long range rifles generously donated by an arms manufacturer. The announcer asked if any of the cultists had any last words. They all chose to remain silent and stared at the mob. As the announcer turned to the hangman, an ear splitting static ripped across the plaza. The crowd pressed their hands against their ears, trying to block the unpleasant sound from hurting their eardrums. It felt like a knife digging deep into them. Harry's radio went haywire and made a variety of strange robotic-like noises until it fell totally silent.

A familiar voice then echoed across the plaza.

"Citizens of Smoke City," the voice growled from the speakers. It was The Leader. He was still alive.

"Before you condemn my children to their deaths. Take a moment to see where you stand. Many of you have never stepped out of the undercity, and here you are, standing toe to toe with your oppressors."

The crowd looked around at each other and at their surroundings.

"The buildings which surround you have dominated your lives for too long. You have a chance now to take them for yourselves, to become equal. The city is weak; its police have been decimated. Use this opportunity to take back what should have been shared amongst you for years."

The Leader continued his speech, and the crowd began to buy into the idea. They became restless and started to express their agreement.

"Harry," Carter said, appearing out of the crowd. "This is happening across the whole city I am being told. Everyone can hear it."

"If this keeps up, there may be a riot."

"There already is in another sector."

"Can we kill the speakers?"

"We are going to have to."

"The time has come, citizens," The Leader continued. "Ahead of you, at City Hall, are this city's so-called powerful: Government officials, company men and bureaucrats. They believe they can subdue you with this charade while they figure out how to cleanse the undercity and send you back down to your miserable existences. Well, I ask, why should you? Why should you return to the dark depths? Why not use this opportunity to establish a new order. A fairer and greater one where you can all be equal?"

The crowd were animated now; they closed towards the support officers who raised their shields and stood firm. Shouts of agreement and approval began to be repeated. The more affluent amongst the crowd tried to slip away unnoticed. A man sporting a monocle and an expensive suit was knocked to the floor. He clambered to his feet and sunk towards the rear of the crowd.

"Take this city back once and for all. Become the city's new children."

One of the crowd members shot forward and fell onto the support officer's heavy shield. He managed to slip the pistol from their holster and fired it in the air. Everyone froze in place, some dropping down to their knees. The man with the pistol then fell to the floor as another deafening crack ripped across the plaza. There was silence for a few seconds before one of the crowd members shouted, "They shot him. The police, they killed him!"

"Yeah," another voice shouted. "Let's do it, let's take this place for ourselves. Come on, everyone!"

The crowd pushed forward and overwhelmed the first line of officers. Others rushed to their aid, trying to stop the surging crowd. The onlookers on the balcony watched as the chaos unfolded below them. The hangman looked at the announcer, confused, not knowing what to do. The announcer didn't know either; instead, he became overwhelmed with panic and retreated towards City Hall.

"Get everyone inside," Carter said down the radio. "Get them inside the building now, we will do what we can out here."

The channel came alive again with radio traffic. Transmissions from confused and panicking officers were broadcast. Harry could hear Harris trying to get control of the situation as he barked orders over the airway, and despite no longer being commissioner he was the only cop everyone would listen to.

"Harry, with me!" Carter shouted from atop the stairs.

Harry took one last look at the angry mob that battled the officers beyond the gallows and followed his boss through the heavy wooden doors and into the building. They slammed shut moments later and were locked tight. The floor they were on contained the main meeting hall for the city's council members. Today the hall was filled with officials, corporate representatives and other wealthy, powerful people who all ran the city in their own self-important way. Many had gathered for a front row seat of the execution like it was some form of sick entertainment. Perhaps it was all they had while their beloved theatres were closed. Harry followed Carter and a group of mildly concerned well-dressed men and women into the main chambers where they took their assigned seats.

The room was filled with hundreds of people. The city's mayor sat at the centre of a long table which was fixed towards the rear of the room. Behind him stood a great mural of the city's skyline. Or at least what it looked like many years ago. Horus Volster sat next to him, seemingly unfazed by the violence beyond the walls. Three other men were also sitting at the desk, sporting similar well-tailored suits. Harry didn't recognise them, although he suspected they were cut from the same cloth as Horus.

Uniformed officers positioned themselves around the building, along with a few detectives. Harris wasn't present. Perhaps he was held up in the command centre trying to get a grip on the deteriorating situation outside of the grand building.

"Harry!" Victoria called.

"Victoria. Please don't tell me you knew that this was your meeting venue."

She marched towards him and seemed out of breath, she brushed her hair aside and said, "I promise you I didn't. Are you sure everyone is safe in here?"

"I don't know. What's the plan if it isn't?"

"I think my brother and a few others have blimps waiting for them."

"Great, another easy target."

"You think the police can stop this riot?"

"I don't know, maybe. The military are meant to arrive anytime now. They should hopefully put an end to it quickly."

"He's still alive, isn't he…The Leader, I mean?"

"I guess so."

Everyone began to take their seats although many remained empty. No doubt some of the guests had decided the situation had become too volatile and had chosen not to remain. The mayor stood up and adjusted his microphone before clearing his throat. He was a short plump man, bald with a red face who had spent years suffering from gout. Harry had never seen him in person but had seen his face on plenty of commercials and posters during his election campaign.

"Ladies and gentlemen," the mayor said, "I assure you the police will have the situation under control, please take a seat and calm down. We will begin the meeting momentarily."

Harry stood at the back of the great room, trying to get a good view of the crowd and those who loitered on the peripheries. Stocky men in suits, likely bodyguards, stood with the uniforms and watched over their employers. Victoria took her seat towards the front of the room; she wasn't on the same table as the mayor but was close enough that she could see the boils on his puffy face.

Harry stuffed his hands in his pockets; he was dying for a cigarette but thought it would be wise to stay focused. As he went to remove his hands, he felt the crunched-up piece of paper he had recovered from the ruined penthouse. He opened it and examined the drawing. The seating arrangement was identical to the one that had been scribbled down. Harry's eyes flicked between the numbers on the paper and the attendees in the immense hall ahead of him. Number one would be Horus, two would be the mayor. Three, four and five would be the other men sat on the table. In the corner of the room, opposite Harry, stood two uniforms. The taller of the pair left his post and lurched towards the mayor and the others. The mayor began his speech and started to detail the great atrocities the city had managed to overcome. Nobody noticed the officers who slowly inched closer to the mayor. Nobody except Harry who bolted down the stairs towards him. The sharpshooters on the upper levels picked up the frantic detective and placed their sights on him. The radio was brimming with chatter, and he couldn't get a word in to warn anyone. The uniforms picked up the pace, the lead unholstering his pistol. Neither wore issued boots, and they were missing their truncheons. Something was amiss and nobody else had noticed it. Harry drew his pistol as he got within distance of Horus. He was sitting far enough away from the mayor so that Harry could shoot between them. As he raised his pistol and got the officer lined up in his sights, he felt a sudden, powerful impact to his back and fell forward in front of the table. A gunshot echoed through the chamber followed by gasps from the attendees. Harry rolled onto his side, thankful that he'd worn the bulletproof vest that Volster had donated to the precinct. Arthur, Horus' aide, walked down the stairs towards him holding his engraved pistol. The sharpshooters didn't know who was a threat and who was simply doing their job, they held their nerve and waited to see what would develop.

"A...Arthur," Harry said, coughing. "They... they aren't cops." He lifted his arm and pointed towards Horus and the mayor.

Arthur, confused to see it was the detective he had shot, looked up at his long-time employer and the two officers behind him. The lead officer raised his gun towards Horus, but Arthur was swifter. He fired two shots that both whizzed past Horus and the mayor and hit the faux officer in the chest. He went down and didn't move again. Another shot echoed through the hall. Arthur hit the floor and landed next to Harry. His eyes remained open; he didn't move nor speak. He had been killed instantly. The sharpshooter on the upper level had seen who he thought was his colleague shot dead, and simply did what he was trained to do. The second imposter, startled by the situation, raised his own revolver and started firing rapidly as he retreated back towards an exit. One of the rounds hit the mayor in the left ass cheek and caused him to let out a high-pitched scream. He leapt forward over the table, knocking over the microphone and his speech notes. Landing on his face, he rolled onto his backside. But that was too painful and made him to scream again so he rolled back onto his fat belly and held his butt cheek in his hands. Horus dived under the table, not wanting to meet the same fate. The sharpshooters were called away to deal with the worsening situation by the front door, reports were coming in thick and fast that the crowd were arming themselves and things could soon become as deadly outside as they were inside.

It was bedlam inside the hall now. Men and women were screaming and bolting up the stairs, desperate to escape the carnage. Harry lifted himself off the floor and onto his knees. Pushing against the other fleeing people was Victoria, adamant that she would make it to the man she loved. The small radio is his jacket pocket was going haywire. Carter was asking for an update and who was shooting who. Harry stared at the city's mayor who was rolling around in pain and screaming for a doctor. Some leader he was. Two detectives, along with his security personnel, rushed to his aid and did their best to drag his fat self into some cover. The pain in Harry's back was severe – he didn't know if he could walk or stand. He felt an arm wrap around his own and panicked, he reached for the pistol that was on the floor by his side and twisted his body.

"Harry!" Victoria shouted. "It's me, it's me."

"God. Arthur…is he?"

"I think so. Come on. On your feet, dammit."

They both groaned as Harry was dragged to his feet. Two more shots ripped across the hall, this time coming from where the imposter had escaped. A tall bald man dressed in a black suit took hold of one of the other men hiding next to Horus under the table. They seemed to recognise one another. Harry realised it was the man's bodyguard and turned to look in the other direction, that was until another gunshot ripped through the air behind him. Harry spun and saw the bodyguard stood over a corpse. He had killed the man he was meant to be protecting. Harry raised his pistol and so did the bodyguard, they exchanged gunfire as Victoria dived for cover. The bodyguard's pistol jammed after being fired twice and Harry used the opportunity to line up an accurate shot. The bullet ripped through the bodyguard's skull and sent him crashing to the floor.

Victoria peaked over a table and said, "Harry. What the fuck is going on?"

The same question was still being screamed over the radio. There were reports of undercover cultists disguised as police officers, bodyguards and emergency workers murdering officials and important figureheads. Some weren't even confirmed to be cultists, they were just people who were sick of being a second-class citizen and bowing to their masters. The situation outside didn't sound much better. The officers were struggling with the crowd and were retreating towards the steep steps which led to the main entrance. If the mob got inside, who knows what they would do or how they would satisfy their rage.

"Quinn!" Horus shouted, his head stuck out from underneath the table. "Get me out of here, will you?"

Horus was frightened, a far cry from his usual confident playboy-like persona which was nothing more than a brittle mask that could easily be smashed when faced with any notion of real danger.

Horus dragged himself out from underneath the table and jogged towards Harry. Victoria joined them both.

"Oh god…Arthur," Horus whimpered, covering his mouth.

Harry grabbed Horus by the collar of his pristine suit and said, "He died defending you, you arrogant piece of shit. If you and the other assholes who run this city had listened in the first place, all of this could have been avoided. He should have let you and our oaf of a mayor take a bullet each."

"Enough, Harry!" Victoria shouted. "Now isn't the time for this. How are we going to get out of here?"

Harry let go of Horus' collar and shoved him away.

Horus flattened his suit down, adjusted his tie and said, "The roof, I have a bird on the roof."

"A bird?" Harry asked.

"Yes, you'll see. Come with me."

"Fine, but we can't take the elevator, it'll be a perfect ambush point."

"Stairs it is."

Harry took one last look at Arthur who lay dead on the base of the stairs. The man had spent his whole life in service of a family that weren't his own. He was a loyal, honourable man who didn't hesitate to defend his employer and gave his life in doing so. There weren't many men like him left in the world.

The trio made their way through the grand hallways of the tower. Harry led from the front, clutching his pistol. Victoria had his revolver and covered their rear. Harry had entrusted her with it as she had proven capable of handling herself. Horus would have to hope that his stepsister and the disgruntled detective would have enough decency to see his escape through to the finish. Dead bodies littered the hallways, some belonging to cultists, others to civilians in suits. One or two uniforms lay dead next to them. Empty shell cases were scattered all over the hard floors and crunched beneath Harry's shoes as he led the group towards the stairwell.

"Harry," Crrzzz, "Harry, it's Carter, do you have an update?" The radio crackled.

Harry stopped and placed the handset to his lips and hit the press to talk button. "I've got Horus, we are making our escape."

"Where are you heading?" a muffled Carter said.

"I won't say. I can't confirm if our communications have been compromised. I'll update you once he is safe."

"Received, watch your back out there. Some of them have disguised themselves as cops; trust nobody, kid."

"I got it."

Harry stuffed the radio back into his pocket. The gunfire which had continuously echoed throughout the building was beginning to cease. Harry wasn't sure if this was a good sign or not, yet he continued to persevere and push onwards. As the group made their way past the elevators, Horus paused at one of the shutters.

"What are you doing?" Harry asked. "I said no elevators."

"I am afraid I won't make it up the stairs, Detective Quinn," Horus moaned. "I think a bullet grazed my leg."

Harry looked down to see blood dripping onto the floor from his right trouser leg.

"The adrenaline is wearing off and I can feel it now."

"Godammit."

Harry's concerns were short lived when two traditionally dressed cultists stepped around the corner, one holding a pump action which he must have taken from a dead officer.

"Into the lift, now!" Harry screamed as he opened fire on the pair and covered their retreat. The cultists dived for cover, the one wielding the shotgun fired blindly but hit nothing but air. The trio ducked into the elevator and Victoria pulled the lever. Next stop, the roof.

CHAPTER TWENTY-THREE

H arry loaded a fresh clip into his pistol and prayed they weren't about to meet their demise when they reached the top of the building. He told the others to hug the walls of the elevator and be prepared for anything. Victoria had ripped her skirt and used the rag to bandage her stepbrother's wounded leg. When the elevator came to a halt, its doors opening presenting an empty corridor, they all relaxed slightly once they saw the coast was clear.

"Let's go," he said, starting towards the door.

Finally outside, they were met with a howl from a powerful gust of wind.

"This way!" Horus shouted, now limping.

He climbed up a metal set of stairs onto the landing pad. Harry was perplexed to see a strange, grey machine. It sported two fan-like thrusters on its wings, and a set of rotor blades were perched atop the main body. Holding the weight of the machine were four mechanical legs. The glass cab contained four seats along with a pilot wearing a flight suit. He sat in the front and looked at the trio with a look of confusion and concern.

"What is this?" Harry asked.

"A New Volster design, called an air hopper. A trial machine for the military so they can get their troops in and out of combat situations quickly. Come on, there are enough seats for all of us."

Horus raised his thumb at the pilot who did the same and then began to fiddle with the controls. A high-pitched whirring sound began to drown out the wind as the blades on top of the contraption began to spin. The turbines on the wings also started to rotate, getting faster with every passing moment. Horus took a step forward and then fell hard onto his face. At first, Harry thought his leg had given way or perhaps he had fainted due to the blood loss. A hole then appeared in the glass cab of the air hopper. The pilot slumped into his seat and stopped fiddling with the controls. Harry turned around to see Esmeralda and Reggie, both disguised as police officers, walking towards them. Neither wore hats, and their tunics were ill fitted and unbuttoned. Esmeralda held a long-barrelled revolver in her hand. Reggie had only a curved knife. She had somehow survived the attack in the undercity and seemed angrier than before.

"Don't make any sudden movements, Detective," Esmeralda commanded as Reggie pulled the gun from Victoria's hand. He stepped behind her and placed the sharp blade against her throat. Victoria froze in fear as she felt the cold metal press against her skin. A thin line of blood, as thick as a blade of grass covered the blade as it dug itself into her flesh.

Raising his arms in desperation, Harry said, "Wait, Reggie, don't do this."

Esmeralda walked towards Harry and snatched the pistol out of his hand and threw it off the edge of the building.

"He won't do anything unless I tell him to," she said.

She then flicked her gun, ushering him to step aside. She raised the revolver towards Horus who tried to roll himself onto his side. She cocked the hammer back and went to pull the trigger but felt her arm jolt upwards as Harry tried to restrain her. She fired a shot into the air and then turned her attention to the detective. Harry threw a straight punch, but Esmeralda dodged it with ease and replied with a kick of her own which caught Harry in the back of the leg. He dropped to one knee and tried to wrestle the gun out of her grip. Esmeralda grabbed her own hand and tried to twist it towards Harry, so the barrel pointed at his face. She cocked the hammer and was about to fire again until she felt her left leg give way. Horus had kicked it out from beneath her as he continued to lie on the ground, doing anything he could to help the dire situation. Wrapping one arm around Esmeralda's hips, Harry lifted her onto his shoulders; he held her other hand tightly so she couldn't move the gun and carried her swiftly towards the now fully spinning turbines. Esmeralda looked over her shoulder to see what awaited her and began to fire blindly in a panic. Neither Reggie nor Victoria had moved during the confrontation, although Victoria could feel that Reggie was beginning to shake, the blade now didn't feel as tight against her neck. One of the rounds ricocheted off the ground near their feet. Reggie panicked and jumped. Victoria used the opportunity and drove her left fist as hard as she could into his groin, hoping it would be enough to disable him. It didn't seem to have the desired effect – Reggie moved but didn't drop to the floor like a normal man should have. Still, it gave her time to break free from his grasp and rush to Harry's aid.

Harry was close to the turbines and could hear nothing but their whining. Another step and he could drop this murderous witch right into them and be done with it all. He felt a sharp red-hot pain run down his shoulder as a bullet ripped through his flesh. The pain was overwhelming, and he fell forward, slamming the cultist down on top of the wing, less than a few feet away from the turbine. She kicked Harry as hard as she could in the face and then raised the revolver towards him. Harry looked straight down the barrel through teary eyes and saw the cylinder rotate. He thought of Caroline and her true, unwavering kindness , then he thought of Victoria and the chaos that had unfolded the past week and how he had stumbled and failed at every hurdle. All his efforts had been for nothing and now he would die on this roof as the city tore itself apart around him. The hammer struck forward but there was no blinding flash nor great beyond. Harry flinched then realised she was empty. Esmeralda pulled the trigger again and again, each time the cylinder rotating but no shot being fired.

"Harry!" Victoria screamed. She rushed to him and pulled him onto his feet and away from the cultist.

Esmeralda looked over beyond the pair and then smiled. Reggie stood behind them both, holding Harry's back up.

"Kill them both, Reggie, do it now," Esmeralda shouted. She tossed the empty gun aside as she pushed herself off the wing.

Victoria held the wounded detective in her arms. Horus continued to lie helplessly on his side and remained silent. He wouldn't have the strength to shout over the near deafening sound of the hopper's engines. Reggie's hand shook as he clutched the revolver. His eyes darted between Esmeralda and the wounded trio.

"Do it!" Esmeralda screamed, taking a step towards him.

"I'm sorry you got involved in all of this!" Victoria shouted.

Reggie struggled to hear her but could roughly make out what she was saying by reading her lips.

"I'm sorry things went the way they did, Reggie. But you are a better man than this!"

"Ignore them, Reggie!" Esmeralda interrupted. "I am speaking on behalf of our leader. Kill them both, now!"

Reggie closed his eyes and cocked the revolver. Esmerelda smiled until she felt a ball of fire rip through her abdomen. She pressed both her hands against the wound and struggled to catch a breath. Harry and Victoria used the opportunity to grab hold of her. Harry throwing as many punches as hard and as fast as he could towards her face, one of them knocking two of her teeth out. Esmeralda did little to defend herself, the pain in her stomach was overwhelming and she had become dazed as the detective struck her repeatedly. She stumbled backwards, trying to stay on her feet. Both Victoria and Harry grabbed a leg each, lifted her off the floor and threw her into the turbine and a spray of blood splattered the grey metallic paintwork. By some miracle, most of it missed them. They both fell to their knees and then looked up at where Reggie had been standing. He was nowhere to be seen. Harry's revolver lay on the floor. The detective dragged himself to his feet and grabbed his piece. Victoria tended to Horus who had gone limp, seemingly succumbing to his wounds.

A huge silhouette appeared in the sky above them, followed by many smaller ones. It was like a flight of dragons or some other otherworldly creatures closing in on them. As the largest silhouette came closer, Harry made out that it was a humongous airplane. It must have had a dozen propellers on either wing. Two plumes of black smoke trailed behind it. A group of smaller, more nimble planes escorted it. Another convoy could be seen in the distance, this one greater than the last. They were heading right towards the centre of the city. The military had finally arrived.

The imposing display of power must have had the desired effect as the rioting groups outside City Hall began to lose their fight upon seeing the giant fortresses soar above them. Several air hoppers painted in a dark green, similar to the one on the building's roof, exited from inside the enormous plane and began to fly in different directions. A group made their way towards the plaza outside of the hall and scattered the crowd. Soldiers, sporting modern tactical gear, their faces concealed by masks with glowing orange eyes, exited the hopper onto the plaza and broke up the crowd with shock sticks and rubber tipped, low velocity rounds. The officers cheered and banged their heavy shields, feeling victorious at last as the raging crowd retreated.

Back on the roof, Harry had managed to shut down the hopper. He flipped every switch to the off position, which eventually killed the engines. He and Victoria sat on the landing pad and admired the display as one plane after the other flew past them.

"Someone must have gotten the word out that the situation had worsened. They wouldn't have arrived like this," Harry said.

Victoria, tearful, wiped her eyes and said, "Let's hope they can gain some control of this city. God, we need a break."

"How's Horus?"

Victoria didn't say anything. She just shook her head and looked up at the grey sky above them as a tear rolled down her cheek.

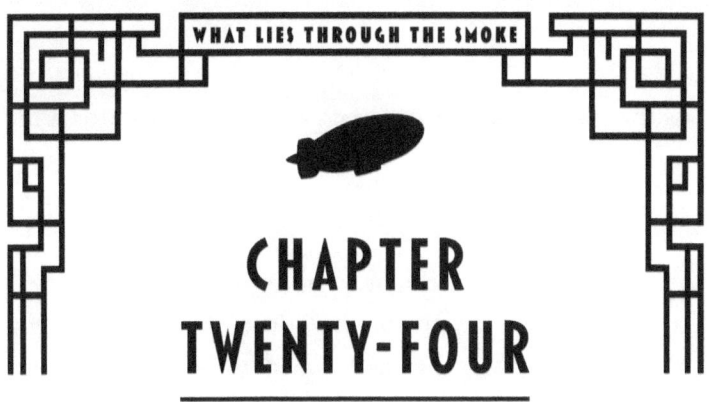

CHAPTER TWENTY-FOUR

The Black Lungs stood ready to ambush the incoming patrol. It would be easy pickings for them as usual. They had all but eliminated the Junkers and almost had total control of the streets; only a few holdouts remained. They stepped out from the alley and saw the figure in a hazmat suit stood in the road. This one looked different from the last. His suit was green and the eyes on his mask glowed a neon orange. No matter, it would still be easy prey. Perhaps he had more to scavenge. The gang took their aim at the figure who stood still in the road and the last thing they heard was a barrage of gunfire ripple down the quiet foggy streets. One of the gang members tried to lift himself off the floor. He looked up through his cracked mask to see tall bi-pedal walkers stomping towards them, each one sporting two machine guns. A metal box protected the driver. The machines put anything his gang had constructed to shame and looked modern and well maintained. Beyond the walkers were row after row of soldiers carrying assault rifles. All with their own glowing orange eyes. The lunger tried to drag himself to his feet but the last thing he saw was the metal claw of a walker crashing down towards him.

***

"There hasn't been a cultist sighting in three days now," Carter said. He reached for the bottle of whisky he kept locked in a drawer beneath his desk. "The army are decontaminating the undercity block by block. Perhaps Volster predicted his zeron would fall into the wrong hands someday, or he simply had it as insurance."

"That's good. The sooner we can get back down there the sooner we can get help to any survivors," Harry said. The bruise around his eye was dark, but the eye itself was slowly becoming a little less bloodshot as each day passed.

Pouring the liquor into two smudged glasses, Carter said, "Agreed, we managed to establish contact with Sergeant Murillo."

"Murillo? I'm glad he made it."

"So am I. He managed to get a few civilians to higher ground away from the gas. He and some other uniforms have been held up for days, fighting off attacks from Black Lungs."

"He's a tough son of a bitch."

"That he is. We still don't know how many died down there, and we still don't know how many we lost. Damn shame about Harris, first day back on the job and he takes one in the back. The mayor made it, because of course he did. But he is now making good on his pledge though and finally throwing more money our way.

Although I suspect the military are going to be here for a little while longer."

Harry took a sip of whisky from a glass and rubbed his face. "I agree. We are going to need them here until things go back to normal. We are going to have to keep flushing out any cultists and see if they have anything else planned."

"You know, the city wasn't far off a full-blown revolution," Carter said, downing the rest of the glass. He leant forward and poured himself another. "But I don't think it was the military's timely arrival that spooked them, you know."

"No?"

"No, I think the people just couldn't quite bring themselves to go through with it. I think The Leader had too much faith in them. Deep down I think folk wanted things to go back to normal. This city has been the same since we were children, and our parents were children. Generations of men and women have born and died in this city and truth be told, it aint changed much. Although I have never seen people turn on their masters like that before. Even some of our own flipped. Everyone's a little on edge and suspicious of each other right now. Going to take some time before the nerves settle."

Harry nodded then said, "I don't think this plan had anything to do with a revolution or balancing the scales?"

"Go on."

"I think it was just an elaborate revenge plot. One that the city would never forget. I don't think The Leader, or the cult, really cared about the people taking back the city. I think he just wanted to destroy those who had wronged him in the past and convinced others to take up his cause. And in truth, they somewhat succeeded."

"Maybe, kid, but they didn't succeed. There is always another corrupt immoral man or woman ready to fill another's shoes. It's just how it is in this city. Horus may be dead, but somebody else will just take his place. We may get lucky, and his sister will step up. I know you are sweet on her, hell I don't blame you either, she's a beaut."

"How many did we lose?"

"Too many, Harry, too many."

"You think we will find The Leader?"

"I don't know, but the feds have asked you join them tomorrow at Proctor's Farm to help with the arrest, seeing as you know exactly where it is and all."

"I'll be there."

"Good, you'll leave here at seven in the morning sharp. They'll give you a ride."

"What's the plan for the rest of the city?"

"Once it's safe to go back, the refugees will return to the undercity. I don't think it'll take much convincing to be honest."

"The city will be back to its crooked ways in no time."

"Perhaps that's how it needs to be, Harry."

"Perhaps."

"We lost a lot of good cops this past week. It's going to take years for the city to recover. The gangs will know it; the people will know it. The Theft department needs a new chief after Cyril turned in his badge – you should apply. I'll put in a good word for you."

Harry couldn't think of anything to say, he just downed the rest of his drink and plonked the glass on Carter's table.

"Go home, get some rest. Be back here first thing tomorrow," Carter said.

Harry grabbed his suit jacket off the seat and stuck his fedora on his head, so it sat at a crooked angle. "I'll let you know what we find out there." The last thing he heard before he left the room was the sound of more liquid flowing as Carter poured himself another glass.

Once Harry was home, he lit a cigarette and stood on his balcony. Things were slowly going back to normal. There seemed to be more life in the city again; a metro train ran across the bridge above his apartment and rattled the empty plates and glasses in his sink. He needed to tidy the place before Victoria returned – if she decided to return, now that all of this was over. There was something he needed to ask her, and he was afraid of the answer. He observed a squadron of military sky hoppers flying in a tight formation between the towers. Technology seemed to be advancing rapidly, and he wondered if he would be able to keep up with the new world.

The hairs stuck up on the back of his neck when he heard a knock at the door. It had almost become the norm that he answered it with a gun in his hand. Victoria was stood outside his apartment staring back at him through the spy hole. He opened the door for her and the two embraced one another. She went to kiss him, but felt that he was withdrawn, and almost cold.

"Harry," Victoria said. "What is it?"

"Come in. There is something I need to ask you."

He shut the door behind her as she hung her coat on the rack.

"What is it? What is it you want to know?"

Harry walked past her towards the kitchen, he turned and placed his gun on the side table, keeping it within arm's reach.

"Jasper didn't kill your father, did he, Victoria?"

"What do you mean?"

"That cut on your arm, the one I treated a few days ago. That wasn't caused by a splinter or something back in the market. It was a clean cut, from a blade. I believe that was from Reggie when you and a cultist paid him a visit. Either to tell him of the plan or to get hold of his uniform. He got scared and tried to defend himself, you tried to calm him down, but he lashed out with a kitchen knife. And you know what? I'm convinced I could smell your perfume in that kitchen. At first, I thought it was from my own clothing but now I'm not so sure."

Victoria stood in silence and just looked down at her feet.

"I think either you sought out The Children, or they sought you out as a way to get close to your father. You lived alone with him in his home, you had his trust so why would he be cautious around you? Then that evening you killed him and stuck the blame on the cult. Jasper even said you knew the real identity of the killer before his brains were splattered back at the precinct. I wonder how that situation would have played out if it hadn't been cut short."

Sighing and taking a deep breath, she turned her green eyes towards Harry and said, "It wasn't the cult. It was Jasper who came to me. He told me that he had a solution to the city's problems. And that with my help he could bring about a great change. Make it so things would be fair and balanced. My father, and other men like him, were in the process of making it even harder for people to get permits to leave the undercity, all while they got richer and fatter. I also found out that my real brother had tried to reach out to me for years after I was adopted, when I was a teenager. Lucius made him disappear. He wasn't a good man, Harry. And...Reggie wasn't meant to be involved. It was Jasper who told me he needed to see him. I wasn't sure why, but I went along anyway. Maybe it was the red cloaks or Jasper's newfound faith, but it spooked Reggie. He went for Jasper; I got in the way and there was a scuffle. Jasper managed to knock Reggie unconscious and got some of his goons to kidnap him, but not before he cut my arm. He stole his uniform and said it was all part of a bigger plan."

"To murder a cop and spook the rest of us, it seems, maybe as a show of their cunning? Was Jasper there as well when you shot him?"

"Yes, he wanted to show Lucius that he was a new man, to try and impress him in some twisted way, although he was far from impressed. He told Jasper he was and always would be a great disappointment to him and the only reason he continued to finance his existence was because it was what his mother would have wanted. Jasper nearly shot him himself until I did . He used the opportunity to promote his cult; said they would take the blame and that this was the first step towards a greater future for Smoke city."

"And you used the opportunity to finally get your revenge. So why did you try to find them afterwards? Why tag along with me?"

"I wanted to see what they were planning, who they were. What kind of people were able to pull my brother away from his miserable life and give him a new wretched purpose. Jasper hadn't told me a lot about his new family, just that I could finally deliver some payback to the man that stole me from my brother and threw me to his own sons like I was their plaything. Besides, Harry, you...I..."

Harry interrupted and said, "Plaything?"

"Horus...he used to..."

"Say no more."

Pacing up and down the living room; she kept her head low . Harry remained still, studying her every move.

"I didn't even know Reggie was alive, that's why I was as startled as you were when we saw him," Victoria said.

"I figured your apology was sincere on that rooftop. What is going to happen with Volster now?"

"They want me as CEO. With Horus dead along with several of the board members, I will look to take charge formally this week. That is, if you don't bring me in."

"I should."

"Will you?"

"I have to, it's my job, Victoria."

"Then perhaps I should choose the alternative option."

Victoria stepped slowly towards the balcony until she held onto the railings. She turned around and leant back on them and stared at the detective.

"Please don't. Whatever you are thinking, don't do it," Harry pleaded, stepping towards her. He couldn't have someone else he cared for die on his watch. There had been too much death for one lifetime, too much life wasted.

"I am not going to spend my life behind bars, Harry. You have given me no other option."

"I'll give you an option."

"Which is?"

"Two days."

"What?"

"I'll give you two days and then I am taking you in. If you choose to remain here in Smoke City or go somewhere else that is up to you. But after those two days, I will look for you."

Victoria contemplated this offer. She had money and resources and was intelligent enough to start again. She stared into the deep brown eyes of the fair and honest man whom she had spent the last week with. She had fallen in love with him, and she knew he had fallen for her. She wasn't sure if Harry was bluffing. Maybe this was his way of offering her another chance.

"I...I... will go...somewhere you won't find me. Somewhere deep inside this city. Back to where I came from."

"Then leave now, don't make me change my mind."

She lifted herself off the cold metal railings and stepped back into the apartment. She gathered her belongings as Harry followed her to the door. Stopping and turning, she kissed him fiercely, wanting to feel his warm embrace should it be her last opportunity to do so. Harry kissed her back and pinned her against the door. Victoria eventually broke free from his lips and stared at him one last time.

"You're a good man, Harry. Caroline was lucky to have you."

Harry said nothing else to the woman walking out of his life. He just stared longingly as she pulled the door shut behind her.

EPILOGUE

A soldier climbed out of the hatch inside the barn at Proctor's Farm, followed by another. Both had modern, compact submachine guns fixed with small telescopic sights slung to their bodies. Many more stood watch around the perimeter of the farm, along with a handful of federal agents. The old V8, which Harry had left abandoned at the farm, had been stripped down and set ablaze. All that remained was a scorched chassis.

"Nothing, sir," a soldier said to their commanding officer who stood next to Harry and a federal agent. The agent sported a typical fed suit, black suit and a black tie. Wanting to let the world know he was a serious man in a dangerous world. Harry couldn't help but laugh to himself when he climbed into the car that morning to leave the city with the agents.

The soldiers all wore hazmat gear as a precaution should any of the zeron gas have been released.

"What was down there, soldier?" the fed asked in a stern voice, wanting to let everyone know he was in charge.

The soldier turned his attention to Harry and the fed, and said, "The gas containers are all still there. But the room where you said they were held up is empty. Been cleared out in a rush though. Still a few personal belongings lying around. The wall of pipes you described was also there, although it looks as if most of the machinery you mentioned is missing. We found this though."

The soldier presented Harry with a white box that was adorned with a red bow. The label said 'Quinn'.

"You want me to open this?" The soldier asked.

"No," Harry said. "Give it to me. I'll open it outside."

He took the box outside of the barn and lifted the lid; inside was a fumer pipe.

"What is it?" the fed asked, trying to steal a peek.

Harry lifted it and inspected it for a couple of seconds before he placed it back into the box.

"It's nothing," Harry said, lighting a cigarette. He took a long drag, probably the longest drag he had ever taken in his life. His mind drifted to Caroline, and then to Victoria. He still hadn't decided whether to pursue her yet. The Volster murder had been officially closed. He held the smoke in his mouth briefly before exhaling. He looked through the cloud of smoke at the intrigued federal agent in the black suit and said, "Nothing but a warning. Or maybe a reminder. Either way, it's going to be a long trip home."

www.ingramcontent.com/pod-product-compliance
Lightning Source LLC
Chambersburg PA
CBHW030248200626
46816CB00002BA/554